GIFTED

Now You See Me

Marilyn Kaye is a bestselling American author. Her Replica series was an international success. Her other series include Camp Sunnyside Friends, After School Club, Out of This World and Last on Earth. She lives in Paris.

Also available:

Gifted: Out of Sight, Out of Mind

Gifted: Better Late Than Never

Gifted: Here Today, Gone Tomorrow

Gifted: Finders Keepers

Gifted: Speak No Evil

GIFTED

Now You See Me

MARILYN KAYE

MACMILLAN CHILDREN'S BOOKS

First published 2010 by Macmillan Children's Books
a division of Macmillan Publishers Limited
20 New Wharf Road, London N1 9RR
Basingstoke and Oxford
Associated companies throughout the world
www.panmacmillan.com

ISBN 978-0-330-51344-9

1 3 5 7 9 8 6 4 2

A CIP catalogue record for this book is available from
the British Library.

Typeset by Ellipsis Books Limited, Glasgow
Printed and bound in the UK by CPI Mackays, Chatham ME5 8TD

For Devlin Burstein

CHAPTER ONE

'TRACEY!'

Her mother's voice rang out loud and clear from the kitchen. Curled up with a book on the living room sofa, Tracey responded.

'What?'

'Tracey! Have you seen my handbag?'

Tracey raised her eyes from the page and surveyed the room.

'It's under the coffee table,' she called back.

'*Tracey!*' Now her mother sounded annoyed. 'Tracey, answer me!'

Tracey frowned. Was her mother developing a hearing problem? She was about to yell back even louder when the front door opened and her father came in and walked right past Tracey without even greeting her. That was when Tracey realized that sometime in the past half-hour, she'd gone invisible.

She wished she could understand how and why this had happened. It used to be so simple. Years of feeling unimportant and not worthy of attention had caused her to go invisible on a regular basis. She didn't feel that way about herself any more, but occasionally she could make herself go invisible by recalling how she used to feel. It wasn't always a reliable process, but she'd been getting better and better at controlling her gift. Still, every now and then it just happened – she would disappear, and she wasn't sure why. Maybe this time it was caused by the book she'd been reading, *Jane Eyre*. The character of Jane had just been sent away to a nasty boarding school, and she was lonely. Maybe Tracey was simply feeling sad for the character . . .

Her father had gone into the kitchen and she could hear her parents' conversation.

'Have you seen my handbag?' her mother asked.

'No, did you lose it?'

'I don't know. I don't think so – I had it this morning. But I've looked all over the house! The seven are at their swimming class, I have to pick them up in ten minutes, and I can't find my bag!'

So *that* was why the house was so quiet, Tracey

mused. Her little sisters, the identical septuplets collectively known as the 'Devon Seven', weren't at home.

'What am I going to do?' her mother wailed. She sounded on the verge of hysteria, which didn't really alarm Tracey. Mrs Devon had a tendency to become terribly dramatic very easily.

Reluctantly, Tracey put her book down. *Come back*, she ordered herself. But of course, it wasn't that easy. She concentrated on feeling good about herself. *People pay attention to me, my parents care about me, I've got friends.* It didn't work – she was still invisible. She really had to work harder on controlling her gift, practise more, learn how to concentrate harder. But meanwhile, her mother needed her handbag.

Tracey got up, retrieved the handbag from under the coffee table, and ambled into the kitchen. Her mother was still ranting.

'My car keys are in the bag! How can I pick the girls up without car keys?'

'Take my car,' Mr Devon suggested.

'But my driver's licence is in my bag! I can't drive without a licence!'

Tracey planted herself in front of her mother and dangled the bag in the air. Her mother didn't blink.

'Where did I leave that bag?' she fretted.

Tracey hadn't been thinking. Of course, if she was invisible, and the bag was in her hands, the bag was invisible too. She dropped the bag on to the kitchen counter.

'Isn't that your bag?' her father asked.

Mrs Devon turned, and gasped. 'It wasn't there two seconds ago!' Then she shrieked. That was when Tracey realized she had become visible again.

This wasn't the first time she'd suddenly appeared in front of her parents, and her parents knew about her so-called 'gift', but her mother couldn't get used to it.

'Tracey, don't *do* that!' she cried out.

'Sorry, Mom, I didn't mean to scare you.' Tracey glanced at the clock on the wall. 'I gotta go — I'm meeting Jenna and Emily at the mall. I'll be home before dinner.'

'But will we actually *see* you later?' her father wanted to know.

Tracey just grinned and took off. She was heading

to the big mall, not the one across from their school, so she had to take a bus. She supposed she could have asked her mother to drop her off on the way to pick up the seven, but she wasn't in the mood to listen to her go on and on about her disappearing act. She had to admit, though, it was kind of nice hearing her parents express a desire to see her. There was a time when that hadn't been the case at all.

Thank goodness she was meeting two friends from her Gifted class, where every student had an unusual skill. Even though their abilities were different, they had some of the same problems. She didn't have to explain or apologize with *them*.

Jenna Kelley and Emily Sanders were waiting for her at their usual meeting place, in front of the bookstore. They made an unlikely pair, Tracey thought as she approached them. Jenna was a goth goddess – black spiky hair with a long fringe that gave her a witchy look. Pale complexion, eyes circled in black kohl, purple lips and a variety of piercings. Black skinny jeans and a black T-shirt with white letters that read 'Stay Out Of My Way'. If you didn't know her, you might think she was dangerous.

Emily's plain long brown hair, soft dreamy expression and unmade-up face made her look at least three years younger than her fourteen years. *Her* jeans were baggy, and her T-shirt was a washed-out pale blue.

And how would Tracey herself fit into the odd combo? As she passed a shop, she glanced at her own reflection in the window and caught a glimpse of a small, slender girl with blonde hair that skimmed her shoulders. Not a lot of make-up – just a little green liner to make her pale eyes sparkle, and a wash of pink gloss on her lips. It was still a pleasant surprise to see how much better she looked now than she used to. Lately, she was happy just to be able to see herself at all.

Her friends were pleased to see her too, though Jenna glanced pointedly at her watch.

'You're five minutes late,' she declared.

Tracey grinned. 'Just be glad I'm here at all. I disappeared for a while today.'

'Without trying?' Emily asked.

Tracey nodded. 'Yeah. It was kind of freaky. Of course, I wasn't as freaked out as my mother was when I reappeared right in front of her. She practically fainted!'

Jenna made a 'humph' sound. 'Serves her right. The way she's treated you, she deserves to be freaked out.'

Tracey brushed that aside. 'That's all in the past, Jenna. And look on the bright side. If my parents hadn't ignored me all those years, I might never have developed my gift.'

'But it still wasn't nice, the way they behaved,' Emily murmured.

She was right, Tracey thought. The Devons had been normal, attentive parents to her when she was very young. But something happened when she turned eight. That was the year the Devon Seven were born.

They weren't the first septuplets in the world, but they were the first identical set of seven girls. Her family became famous, and Tracey could remember being just as excited as everyone else about the remarkable birth of her sisters. But then things changed.

She supposed it was normal for her parents to become completely preoccupied with the newborn girls. But was it normal for them to completely forget their oldest child?

It wasn't like those terrible stories of child abuse you read about in newspapers. They didn't yell at

Tracey, or hit her, or refuse to give her food. It was more like Tracey just wasn't there any more, like she'd ceased to exist. And Tracey found herself responding by simply fading away.

At first, it was just in her mind – it was her own attitude that made her feel 'invisible' to people outside her own family. If she didn't deserve attention at home, why should she expect anyone else to notice her? That was the kind of vibe she gave off, and people reacted by not giving her any consideration. At school, teachers never called on her. On the street, people would bump into her and then look surprised, as if they hadn't realized anyone was there. In shops, she couldn't get a salesperson to wait on her.

It got worse and worse. Since no one seemed to care about her, she stopped caring for herself. And as bizarre as it sounded, it seemed inevitable that she would become physically, as well as emotionally, invisible.

But all that had changed. Tracey had learned to assert herself and demand the attention she deserved as a human being. She could still disappear, sometimes on purpose, but she didn't have complete control over her gift. Neither did Emily or Jenna, but they were all learning more and more about what they could do. Emily had learned how to examine her visions of the future, so she could understand what she was actually seeing. As for Jenna . . .

'Read any interesting minds lately?' Tracey asked her as they strolled through the mall.

'Nothing worth talking about,' Jenna said. 'But I was thinking, the other day – you know what would be cool? If I could hang out at police stations and check out all the people who are arrested, and tell the cops whether or not they really committed any crimes. Or go to trials and read the minds of the defendants. I'd be able to tell the judge if they were guilty or not, and they wouldn't even need a jury.'

'Dream on,' Tracey commented. 'You think the judge would believe you?'

'And since when do you want to help police officers?' Emily wanted to know. 'You're always saying you don't like cops.'

'And even if the police believed you, Madame would *kill* you,' Tracey added.

Jenna made an elaborate 'who cares' gesture. 'Big deal.'

Tracey and Emily exchanged knowing glances. Jenna liked to act tough, as if she wasn't scared of anything or anyone, but her friends knew better. All the students in the Gifted class had a healthy respect for Madame. She was one of the few people they could totally trust with the knowledge of their gifts, and the only one who really understood the gifts and what they meant.

Madame was always telling them to keep their gifts secret, and for good reason. They'd all had experiences with some real low-life types who wanted to use their abilities for less-than-noble purposes.

Jenna glared at them both. 'I know what you're thinking.'

Emily gave her a reproving look. 'Jenna, you're not supposed to try to read our minds.'

'Didn't have to,' Jenna declared. 'It's all over your faces – you think I'm showing off. But I'm telling you, I don't care what Madame thinks.'

'And you'll never know, will you?' Tracey said. 'You can't read Madame's mind, right?'

'Not if she knows I'm around,' Jenna replied. 'You know, I've finally figured out why some people are a total blank to me. If they know what I can do, they can figure out how to block their thoughts from me. That's why I could never read my mother's mind. She always knew about me.' She sighed. 'I used to think it was because we're related. And I thought that was why I couldn't read that – that man's mind. Because I believed he was my father.'

Tracey knew who she was talking about. A man had turned up one day over a month ago and claimed he was Jenna's long-lost father. At first she believed him, and she was thrilled. But he wasn't her father; he was no relation to her at all. Somehow, he'd learned about her gift. And all he really wanted was for Jenna to read minds for him so he could win at poker.

'He knew what you could do so he blocked you,' Emily said.

Jenna nodded. 'What I always wondered was, how did he find out about me?'

Neither Tracey nor Emily could answer that. And Tracey was more interested in learning something else.

'So, how do we block you?'

Jenna grinned. 'You'll have to figure that out for yourselves.'

'It's easy,' Emily informed Tracey. 'I've been

practising. You get the feeling she's poking around in your head and you just shut her out. It's like an instinct or something.'

Jenna gave her a sour look. 'Thanks a lot. I don't care, anyway. I mean, it's not like you two ever think about anything worth hearing.'

'That's right,' Tracey said cheerfully. 'Besides, we always end up telling each other what we're thinking.'

'That's true,' Emily noted. And even Jenna had to agree with that.

Tracey agreed too, and she felt pretty good about it. It was *nice* having friends she could be so open with, friends who understood what you were all about. Their parents knew about their special talents, but they couldn't really understand, since they didn't have these gifts themselves. That was what made the Gifted class so special. They could talk freely about their abilities and everyone could relate to them. They could be appreciated and respected by each other.

OK, maybe 'everyone' was an exaggeration. Tracey spotted someone just a short distance in front of them who'd never expressed much appreciation or respect for any of her classmates.

Jenna saw her too, and groaned. 'Uh-oh, watch out. The Evil Queen and her Evilettes are here.'

Amanda Beeson was looking into the window of a new boutique, Apparel, with her pals Nina and Britney.

'Gee, from a distance, they almost look like human beings,' Jenna commented.

'Oh, come on, Jenna, they're not that bad,' Tracey remonstrated. 'OK, Nina and Britney are pretty snotty, but Amanda can be OK sometimes.'

'Yeah? Like when?'

Tracey turned to Emily. 'Don't forget, she was the one who saved you when you were trapped in the closet at school with that awful Serena. Remember?'

Emily shuddered. 'I'm not likely to forget *that*. But it wasn't Amanda who burst into the closet, it was *you*.'

Tracey shook her head. 'Amanda had taken over my body, and she was in control. So it was really her.'

'Oh yeah, that's right,' Emily murmured.

'I don't care, I think she's positively despicable,' Jenna declared. 'She didn't do a thing to help Ken in that seance scam, remember?'

It was less than two weeks ago, so Tracey wasn't likely to have forgotten the event already – they'd been discussing it ever since. Ken's so-called 'gift' was the ability to communicate with dead people. Looking for someone who might understand what he could do, he'd got involved with a fake medium. Amanda had taken over the body of another seance participant. Amanda could only do this when she felt sorry for someone, so this woman must have seemed pretty sad. But even when Amanda learned that the participant was the medium's partner-in-crime, she'd done nothing to stop the scam from moving on.

'That was pretty weird,' Tracey admitted. 'Especially because I always thought Amanda was into Ken.'

'Amanda is into Amanda,' Jenna declared. 'It must have been really horrible for you, having Amanda in your head.'

'I don't know,' Tracey answered honestly. 'I don't remember anything. It's like I was asleep.'

'She'd better not ever try to take over my body,' Jenna declared.

'I doubt that could happen,' Emily said. 'She has to feel sorry for someone before she can take over their body. Why would she ever feel sorry for you?'

'Because I can't afford the clothes in Apparel,' Jenna

replied. 'Not that I'd ever want any of them. And you know what? I don't buy that business, about Amanda feeling sorry for people. She's a selfish snob and she never thinks about anyone but herself.'

'That's not true,' Tracey said. 'When she had my body, she did a lot for me. She got my parents to pay attention to me. She bought me decent clothes, she got me a haircut . . .'

Jenna snorted. 'Only because she was afraid she'd be stuck being you for ever.'

Tracey wasn't so sure about that. Even though she hadn't been aware of Amanda's intentions when Amanda was inhabiting her body, she couldn't help feeling the girl might have had some kind motives. She was about to tell Jenna this when she noticed that Jenna was staring at Amanda in a particular way that Tracey recognized.

'Are you reading her mind?' Tracey asked.

'Yeah, she's thinking about trying on the skirt in the window. Thrilling, huh?' But then her expression changed. 'Whoa, wait a second.'

'What is it?' Emily asked.

'She's got a secret. It's . . . it's something to do with,

15

with . . .' she squinted in her effort to concentrate. Then her eyes widened in surprise. 'She's thinking about Mr Jackson!'

Tracey was startled. 'As in Principal Jackson?'

'What kind of secret could she have about Mr Jackson?' Emily wanted to know.

They weren't going to find out – at least, not that day. Amanda spotted them.

'Damn, she's learned how to block me too,' Jenna muttered.

Tracey laughed. 'What did you think she'd do? "Hi, Jenna, welcome to my private thoughts."' She smiled at Amanda, but all she got back was a blink of recognition before Amanda moved hurriedly away, with Nina and Britney at her heels.

'She really is a snob,' Emily remarked. 'She won't even speak to us.'

'It's just because she's with her friends,' Tracey said. 'She knows Nina would say something nasty to us. I think she's trying to protect us from being insulted.'

Both Jenna and Emily gazed at her as if she was out of her mind.

'Why are you always defending her?' Jenna asked.

'I don't know.' Tracey sighed. 'I guess I can't help thinking there's something good in Amanda.' The expressions of disbelief on her friends' faces remained intact, so she changed the subject.

She turned to Emily. 'Got any predictions to make?'

'About what?' Emily asked.

'Anything.'

'It doesn't work like that,' Emily said. 'I have to be thinking about something in particular.'

'Think about me,' Jenna suggested. 'Is anything interesting going to happen to me this week?'

Obediently, Emily looked at Jenna in that peculiarly dreamy way she took on when she was trying to get an image of the future. Her eyes glazed over.

'Well?' Jenna asked impatiently. 'Can you see me?'

'Yes.' Emily's brow furrowed. 'With . . . with a knife in your hand.'

'Good grief!' Tracey exclaimed. 'Is she pointing it at someone?'

'No. She's just holding a knife.'

Tracey looked at Jenna worriedly. After all, her friend did have a reputation. When she'd first come to Meadowbrook straight from some sort of place for delinquent teens, she'd been observed with trepidation by students and teachers.

Jenna just shrugged. 'That makes sense.'

'It does?' Emily asked. Now she was looking nervously at Jenna too.

Jenna nodded. 'I'm fixing dinner tonight, and I'm making tuna salad. I'll be chopping onions, celery, carrots . . . yeah, I guess I'll be holding a knife for at least half an hour.'

Tracey immediately felt guilty for having even considered that Jenna might be planning to do something criminal with a knife. Jenna didn't hang with gangs any more, and even though she retained her tough-girl demeanour, she hadn't been in any serious trouble. Tracey was absolutely, positively, no-doubt-about-it certain that Jenna had completely reformed.

Still, it was reassuring to know that Jenna's knife would be used for strictly non-violent purposes.

Chapter Two

WHAT A DIFFERENCE a few months could make, Jenna thought as she strolled into Room 209 on Monday afternoon. She remembered the first day she'd entered this classroom, and how angry, depressed and scared she'd been. She'd just been let out of that place she'd been sent to after her arrest for drug possession. Harmony House . . . a fancy name for what was really a jail for teenagers. She'd been taken away from home and forced to spend three months with thieves, gang leaders, addicts . . . when *her* only real crime had been hanging with people like that.

Not that home was such a great place to be either. Her mother was rarely there, and when she *was* at home, she was drunk. Welfare cheques were spent on booze and who-knew-what-else, and Jenna could recall many nights when she went to bed hungry.

So release from Harmony House wasn't any great relief. She went back to Brookside Towers, the nasty low-income housing development she'd been living in with her mother for two years. Her mother was still drinking, still partying. The apartment was a mess, her *life* was a mess, and she had to keep that fact a secret from the social workers or she'd be sent into foster care.

By order of the judge, Jenna had been transferred to this school, Meadowbrook, and as if that wasn't bad enough, she also had to report to a school counsellor every week. But the counsellor, Mr Gonzalez, wasn't such a bad guy. He didn't know about Jenna's ability to read minds, but he must have suspected there was something uniquely odd about her because he sent her to see Madame. Jenna had been furious – she'd been branded as a 'problem' again and now she had to attend a 'special' class with other problem students.

So the first time she entered this classroom, she was in a very bad mood. The so-called 'Gifted' class could only make her already wretched life even worse.

But then things began to turn around for her. Aspects of her life started to improve. Her mother went into a rehab programme, and now she'd been sober for over a month. She'd got a job too.

Even her home was better. The residents of Brookside Towers were demanding long-overdue improvements to the estate, and the local government was actually responding.

And the Gifted class turned out to be nothing like what she'd expected. Her classmates weren't 'problems' – not in the traditional sense. They had 'gifts' too. And despite her usual efforts to remain aloof and disagreeable, Jenna found herself fitting in – and even making friends. It wasn't in Jenna's nature to show her feelings or admit them to anyone, but deep in her heart she knew she was as close to being happy as she'd ever been.

Not that she was great friends with *all* her classmates. She glanced at Martin Cooper, who sat over by the windows. He was looking at her right now with fear in his eyes.

'You'd better not be reading my mind,' he said to her in an accusing tone.

Jenna shook her head wearily. The little wimp couldn't even figure out how to block her. He was the eternal victim, always expecting to be picked on and bullied. His only satisfaction came when he was teased so much that his gift emerged – and an incredible physical strength made him capable of causing serious damage.

'Out of my way,' barked a voice behind her. Jenna stayed right where she was, knowing full well that Charles Temple could easily manoeuvre his wheelchair around her. She wondered if being unable to walk was the reason he could be so aggressive and argumentative. She assumed it was the source of his gift – telekinesis – the ability to make things move with his mind.

Sarah Miller was already in her seat, of course. Jenna always thought of her as 'Little Miss Too Good to Be True'. How else could she criticize someone who was always sweet? It was still hard to believe that Sarah had potentially the most dangerous gift of all of them – the ability to make people do anything she wanted them to do. Not that Jenna had seen much evidence of this amazing gift. For some mysterious reason, Sarah didn't want to use her talent.

Ken Preston looked up and caught her eye. 'Hi,' he

said. The greeting wasn't expressed very warmly, but Jenna was just pleased to be acknowledged by him. She and Ken had experienced some conflicts recently, and she didn't want him to hold anything against her. He wasn't a close friend like Emily or Tracey, but she thought he was an OK kind of guy. Also, since that seance experience, he was pretty down on Amanda, and any enemy of Amanda's was a friend of hers.

She plunked down in the seat next to him. 'Hi. What's up?'

'Not much,' he said. 'You?'

'Nothing special,' she replied. They both fell silent. Jenna tried to think of a way to keep the conversation going.

'Heard from anyone interesting lately?' she ventured.

He seemed to be considering the question. 'Well, there's this lady who was watching some series on TV before she died, and she's always asking me to find out what's happening on it. So I started watching the show, but it's really stupid and I hate it.'

Jenna shrugged. In her opinion, Ken was just too nice to the dead people who communicated with him. Of all the gifts, Ken's was the one she'd least want to have. 'So tell her to leave you alone.' She turned away from him, and pretended to gasp. 'Hey, what's Carter doing?'

Ken's eyes widened and he turned swiftly to look at the boy who sat at the back of the room. 'What are you talking about?'

Jenna grinned. 'Gotcha.'

Carter Street was the mystery of the Gifted class, a mute, blank-eyed boy who seemed to be more of a robot than a human being. He did what he was told to do, but he never responded or took any initiative, and his expression was always the same – empty. No one knew his real name or where he came from, or if he had any kind of gift at all. Jenna wasn't even sure what he was doing in the class.

Emily and Tracey came in, but Jenna couldn't say anything more than 'Hi' because Madame was right behind them, and the bell rang. Madame took her usual place behind her desk at the front of the room, and she gave them her usual smile of greeting – but the smile looked a little tense to Jenna.

Her eyes scanned the room. 'Where's Amanda?' she asked.

Nobody responded, and Madame frowned. She was big on punctuality.

'I've got a task for you today,' the teacher continued. As usual, there were a couple of groans, and as usual, Madame ignored them. 'I want each of you to make a list of all the people who know about your gift. Include parents, and any other family member who is aware of what you can do.'

'Why?' Ken wanted to know.

Jenna half-expected Madame to snap something like 'because I told you to' – but that was how other teachers would respond to a question like that. Madame wasn't like other teachers.

She seemed to be taking her time, and considering her answer carefully. Finally, she spoke.

'It's important for all of us to be aware of who knows about the gifts. You all know by now that there are people out there who want to use you, to utilize your gifts for their own purposes. We have to keep track of all potential . . . potential problems.'

'But you said we have to include our parents,' Sarah said. 'You don't think *they'd* want to use us, do you?'

'Not intentionally,' Madame said quickly. 'But

they might slip and reveal something to someone who – who shouldn't know about you. They may already have done so.'

'Why do you think that?' Tracey asked.

'Because you've all had experiences which lead me to believe that you've been observed. That you're being watched.'

Martin went completely white. 'You mean, someone's spying on us?' He looked around nervously. 'Right now?'

At that moment, the door opened and Amanda walked in. Actually, sauntered in would be a better way of describing her entrance, Jenna thought. Most students entering a classroom late would shuffle in with head down. Amanda was practically strutting.

Madame looked at her, and raised her eyebrows. Amanda smiled brightly, and didn't even bother to apologize for her tardiness.

'I have an excuse,' she proclaimed, and handed a folded piece of paper to the teacher.

Madame opened the note, and looked at it.

'I can't read this signature,' she said.

'It's from Mr Jackson,' Amanda said. 'I've been

working in the office. You see, I'm his new student assistant.'

Jenna couldn't blame the cool, calm and collected teacher for becoming momentarily speechless. This was pretty shocking news, considering who it was coming from. Jenna knew of other students who worked as assistants – in the cafeteria, the gymnasium, and the library. But Amanda Beeson was the last person in the world who would be expected to take a job like that. Students did jobs like this to get extra-curricular credits, or build up experiences that would make it easier to get part-time paying jobs when they were in high school. Amanda was only interested in social extra-curricular activities, and it was unlikely that she'd be thinking about working for money when she got into high school. Her parents were either rich or very generous. In any case, Amanda certainly didn't need to work for spending money.

She assumed Madame was thinking the same thing. 'Why have you suddenly decided to become a student assistant, Amanda?'

Clearly, Amanda hadn't anticipated the question. 'I . . . I just think it's good to learn office skills,' she finally replied. 'I mean, you never know when you might, um, need them.'

Madame eyed her curiously, but she didn't press the issue. 'Take a seat, Amanda,' Madame said. 'And please make it clear to Mr Jackson that I expect my students to be here on time.'

Jenna and Emily exchanged looks. They knew why Madame sounded a little huffy about Mr Jackson. She hadn't been too thrilled when the principal foisted a student teacher on the class. Especially when that student teacher turned out to have aspirations other than teaching . . .

Madame repeated the day's assignment to Amanda, and everyone went to work on their lists. Jenna's was pretty short. There was her mother. She was pretty sure her mother wouldn't have told anyone else, even if she was drunk. And then there was that man who called himself Stuart Kelley and claimed to be the father she'd never known. He could have told other people, she supposed. But how many people would believe someone who claimed he knew a mind-reader? That was the benefit of having the kind of weird talents they all had – people didn't believe their gifts were possible.

She added names she was pretty sure were on everyone's list – the people who had tried to force some of her classmates to rob banks for them. Clare, and those two men who'd been with her. Serena, the student teacher, of course. But that was about it. She'd never told any of the cops, or social workers, or judges she'd encountered in her brief career as a juvenile delinquent. Or any of the foster families she'd been forced to live with back when her mother went on one of her binges.

Madame collected the lists, and they spent the rest of the class time discussing the names on them.

'Charles, you have two brothers in high school,' Madame noted. 'Do you think that they might talk about you with their friends?'

'No,' Charles said. 'They're ashamed of me.'

Madame looked at him doubtfully, but she didn't pursue the subject. 'I see that all of you put Ms Hancock on your lists,' she commented.

'I didn't,' Jenna protested. 'Who's Ms Hancock?'

'Serena, the student teacher,' Sarah reminded her.

'Oh, OK, I forgot her last name. If it *is* her real last name.'

'You shouldn't forget anything about that woman,' Madame warned her. 'She's dangerous. She learned about your gifts when she was here. And she utilized that knowledge to get Ken involved in that seance scam.'

Jenna didn't miss the way Ken shot a dark look at Amanda before responding to Madame's comment.

'There's something I still don't understand about that,' he said. 'I know she was the one who invited me to the seance. But what I can't figure out is how she got the invitation into my locker. We've got pretty tight security here. It's not like someone can just walk into the school and put notes in lockers.'

'Maybe she got someone to do it for her,' Emily suggested. 'Someone who could get past security. Someone who actually belongs here.'

A silence fell over the room, and Jenna assumed her classmates had the same thought running through their minds as she had. The bell rang.

'We'll continue this discussion tomorrow,' Madame said, and dismissed them.

Outside the classroom, Jenna paused at the water fountain. Emily and Tracey waited for her, and Ken joined them.

'What do you think?' Ken asked the girls. 'Is there a spy at Meadowbrook?'

Emily considered this. 'It seems to me that if one student knew about us, everyone would know about us. You know how rumours spread around here.'

'Not necessarily,' Jenna remarked. 'Not if that student wanted to do something more important than just spread gossip about us. Like, pass information to our enemies.'

'Exactly,' Ken said. 'If someone is working with *them*, she wouldn't want other kids at school to know what she knows.'

Tracey frowned. 'Why do you think it's a "she"?'

Ken shrugged, and didn't answer, but Jenna read his mind before he could block her. 'You think Amanda's the spy.'

'That's ridiculous,' Tracey said. 'Why would Amanda do something like that?'

'Maybe because she's a terrible person?' Jenna suggested. 'Maybe because she's a snob who thinks she's better than the rest of us?'

'It's gotta be someone in our class,' Ken said. 'No one else could know so much about us.'

Tracey shook her head. 'You think we're the only ones who know where your locker is, Ken? I've seen you hang around there with your pals. Maybe one of them is working with Serena and put her note in your locker.'

'But does anyone else know that Jenna's father disappeared before she was born?' Ken asked.

Jenna shook her head. 'So that guy who said he was my father had to learn about me from someone in our class.'

'That still doesn't mean the spy is Amanda,' Tracey pointed out.

'She knew Serena was posing as Cassandra-the-medium and she didn't tell anyone,' Ken offered.

'Maybe she was afraid of Serena,' Tracey murmured.

'She's working in the office,' Emily pointed out.

'So what?' Tracey asked.

Jenna answered for Emily. 'So she has access to all kinds of personal information about us. I'll bet that's why she took the job, so she could pass it on.'

Tracey groaned. 'Come on, you guys, you're just ganging up on Amanda because you don't like her.

OK, maybe someone in our class is a spy. Let's think of who else it could be.'

Emily spoke. 'Martin?'

Ken looked at her in disbelief. 'That weasel? He wouldn't have the guts.'

'I'm not so sure about that,' Tracey said. 'All that "scaredy-cat" stuff could be a big act. He's totally self-centred. Remember when we were kidnapped? He was completely willing to go along with those guys. I think he'd sell us out to anyone who paid attention to him.'

'I guess you've got a point,' Jenna said grudgingly.

But Ken was more stubborn. 'I still think it's Amanda.'

'Whoever it is, we need to know,' Jenna declared. 'So what are we going to do?' She looked at Tracey. 'You got any ideas?'

Tracey nodded. 'I think I'm going to do a little spying myself.' She grinned at the others briefly, and then scrunched her face, as if she was concentrating very hard.

And before their very eyes, she disappeared.

Chapter Three

SOMETIMES IT WORKED, JUST like *that*. Would she ever figure out the logic of her gift? Tracey couldn't take time to think about it now, she had to move. Fortunately, Martin was a slow walker, and she caught up with him just outside the school. Of course, he had no idea she was walking alongside him. Tracey was pretty sure Martin hardly ever had anyone *visible* walking beside him never mind *invisible*.

She'd never seen him hanging about with other kids at school. She supposed that wasn't so weird – after all, until a couple of months ago, Tracey didn't hang out with anyone at school either. She'd been as much of a loner as Martin seemed to be. But there'd been good reasons for Tracey's isolation.

Maybe Martin had reasons too, but maybe they were bad ones. Maybe right this minute he was on his way to meet Serena, or Clare the kidnapper, or some other person who was interested in gifted students for all the wrong reasons.

If so, Martin wasn't in any rush to get there. He walked slowly, head down, shoulders slumped, dragging his feet.

As they walked, Tracey took the time to give Martin a long, hard look. She'd never paid much attention to him in class – he was so irritating, everyone tried to ignore him. But now that he was silent, she was able to actually *see* him – and she was mildly surprised by what she saw. Physically, he really wasn't that awful.

Whenever she envisioned Martin – which wasn't often – she always thought of him as being a puny kid, sort of a less-than-lifesize scarecrow. But she realized now that he'd been growing, and he was several inches taller than she was. He was thin, but not totally scrawny. His hair was still fair, but he couldn't have had a haircut recently. The straight blond strands fell down his forehead and almost into his eyes. Which were very green – funny how she'd never noticed that before. If she hadn't known him, she'd almost think he was kind of cute.

But she *did* know him – he was Martin Cooper, whiny and fussy and annoying. And possibly a traitor to his class.

On a leafy, residential street, he turned and made his way up the drive of a house. A plump fair-haired woman was on the front steps, and she looked anxious. When she spotted Martin, she hurried forward.

'There you are, honey! You're late, I was getting worried.' She enveloped Martin in a tight hug.

Well, he was loved, Tracey thought. Clearly, he didn't have the kind of problems Tracey used to have. But what was all this business about being late? OK, Martin had walked slowly, but he'd come directly home.

Mrs Cooper ushered her son into the house and Tracey followed close behind.

'You know how I worry when you're late,' the woman said to Martin.

'I'm not late,' Martin protested weakly.

'You're usually here at three thirty-five,' his mother said. She looked at her watch. 'It's three forty-two!'

Seven minutes late, Tracey thought. This lady was kind of obsessive. She looked around the living room they were walking through. Everything looked very clean and neat. There was a sofa, easy chairs, the usual stuff – the only things in the room that seemed a little odd were the pictures on the walls. They were all photos of Martin, from birth to his most recent school picture.

He was an only child, that much was obvious. In a few of the pictures, Martin was posing with his mother, but there was no sign of a father. Was Mrs Cooper a widow or divorced? Divorced, Tracey decided. Otherwise, there'd be some indication of the other person who'd helped to produce Martin.

Pleased with the conclusions she'd come to by way of observation, Tracey was beginning to think she might make a pretty good spy. She followed Martin and his mother into a large, country-style kitchen.

'Wait till you see the snack I have for you today!' Mrs Cooper announced. She lifted the lid off a cake tin. 'Chocolate with butterscotch icing! What do you say to that?'

'Thank you, Mom,' Martin said automatically, but there wasn't a lot of enthusiasm in his tone. He allowed his mother to lead him to a chair at the kitchen table and practically place him on it. Then she stepped back and gazed at him worriedly.

'You're looking a little pale, darling. Have you got a fever?' She placed a hand on his forehead. Martin flinched, but he didn't push the hand away. Finally, his mother removed it. 'No, I don't think so. But I want you to take it easy today, dear. No running around, all right? You know how sport tires you out. You're just not suited to it.'

Good grief, Tracey thought. This woman wasn't just a little obsessive, she was a nervous wreck.

Martin picked up the knife that lay next to the cake tin and started to cut a slice of cake. His mother squealed.

'Honey, be careful! That's a very sharp knife. Here, let me cut the cake for you. There's milk in the refrigerator.'

Martin relinquished the knife to his mother, got up and went to the refrigerator. Back at the table, he looked at the unopened carton of milk for a few seconds, and then touched the cap.

'I can't get this open,' he whined.

'You didn't even try!' Tracey exclaimed, forgetting that no one could hear her.

'I'll do it for you,' his mother said.

She treats him like a baby, Tracey realized. So that's how he acts. This was confirmed to her when his mother unfolded a napkin and actually tucked it into his neckline, like a bib. And Martin let her.

While Martin ate, his mother hovered over him and kept up a non-stop stream of chatter. 'Now, when you've finished with your snack, we'll go to the supermarket. Unless you're too tired, of course. But we're almost out of the cookies you like so much. And maybe we can stop at the hair salon – your grandfather keeps telling me your hair is too long.' She leaned over and brushed a lock off his forehead. 'Though I think it looks sweet. I remember your first haircut, when you were two. I cried!'

Tracey was beginning to feel nauseous. This was too, too sickening.

When he finished his snack, Martin made no move to take his plate and glass off the table. Why should he? His mother automatically took them away and began washing them at the sink. Without even thanking her, Martin got up and went into the living room. Tracey followed him.

He plunked himself down on the sofa, picked up a remote control from the coffee table, and pointed it towards the TV. Tracey was surprised to see that he surfed the channels all by himself, and didn't demand that his mother do it for him.

He let the screen rest on what looked like a rerun of an old series. After a few minutes of watching it with him, Tracey recognized it – 'The Incredible Hulk'. That figured. Martin would appreciate the story of an ordinary man who could turn into a violent superhero.

The front door opened, and a man came in. Martin's eyes didn't leave the screen, but Tracey looked at the newcomer with interest. He seemed pretty old, with hair that was almost completely white and a lot of lines on his face. But he looked like he was in good shape, and when he spoke, his voice was strong.

'Can't you even say "hello" to your grandfather, boy?'

Martin's lips formed the shape of 'Hi' but Tracey couldn't hear anything. Mrs Cooper came into the room.

'Hi, Dad. Martin, are you ready to go to the supermarket? Oh dear, you *do* look tired. Maybe you should stay at home. Dad, could you watch Martin while I do some shopping?'

'Good grief, Linda,' the man said. 'He's almost fourteen years old! He doesn't need babysitting.'

The woman gazed at her son fondly. 'He'll always be my baby. Well, I'm off – back in an hour or so.'

Once she'd left, the man took the remote control and switched the TV off.

'Hey, I was watching that,' Martin protested.

'It's too nice outside to be watching television,' his grandfather replied. 'Let's go kick a ball around in the back yard.'

'I don't want to go outside,' Martin said.

'C'mon, it's good for you.'

'I'm tired,' Martin whined.

'Don't give me that nonsense,' the man barked. 'You're too young to be tired.'

'But Mom said—'

'I don't care what your mother said! Get your lazy butt off that couch and come outside with me!'

Martin blanched, and Tracey flinched. She could sort of understand the man's frustration with Martin, but he could have been a little gentler in his persuasion methods.

At least he'd scared Martin into getting up. Tracey followed them through the kitchen and out the back door. The grandfather jogged over to the ball lying on the grass, and kicked it in Martin's direction. When it flew past him, Martin ducked and made no effort to go after it.

'Kick it back!' the old man ordered him.

Slowly, Martin ambled towards the ball.

'Run!' his grandfather yelled.

Martin may have picked up the pace a bit, but any increase in speed was imperceptible to Tracey. And when he reached the ball, he barely tapped it with his toe.

'You call that a kick? Put some muscle into it!'

This time the ball actually moved a few feet. The man ran towards it, and gave it a fierce kick. The ball hit Martin in the stomach, and Martin let out an ear-shattering wail.

'Ow, that hurt!'

Tracey couldn't tell if Martin was really suffering or if he was just putting on one of his acts. In any case, it made no difference to the grandfather.

'Stop complaining, you little brat! You're a big baby. Grow up, you stupid child!'

Martin froze. The man continued with his tirade.

'You know what? You're pathetic! How did I end up with such a lousy grandchild? You make me sick!'

Tracey watched Martin in alarm. The boy was becoming flushed and his breathing had become so laboured she could hear it from where she was standing at the edge of the yard. Then his whole body began to tremble.

She knew what this meant. Martin's gift was emerging, just as it always did when he was teased or taunted. Frantically, she turned to the grandfather. Was he aware of Martin's ability? Did he know that any minute now Martin would be able to beat the man to a pulp?

And what should *she* do? How could she stop Martin, rescue the old man, put an end to this? Madame could control Martin with a sharp look, but Tracey wasn't Madame. Besides, Martin wouldn't even be able to see any sharp look Tracey could muster!

But to her amazement – and relief – Martin didn't explode into a fury of super strength. She watched with interest as his face contorted into an expression of intense concentration. And after a moment, his complexion returned to its normal colour, his breathing calmed, and his body was still. Then he ran back into the house.

Now she was confused. Why hadn't Martin attacked the man? Was he able to control his gift? She wished Jenna was there. She could have read Martin's mind and explained why he was acting like this.

The back door had been left open, so Tracey didn't have to wait for the grandfather to let her back inside. She hurried after Martin.

He wasn't in the kitchen or the living room, so she went upstairs. In the hallway she could hear sobs coming from behind a closed door. Usually, Martin's self-pitying tendencies annoyed her. This time, to her surprise, she found herself feeling sympathy for him.

As long as the door remained closed, however, there was nothing she could do about it. She couldn't walk through walls. She'd just have to wait for Martin to come back out.

Fortunately, he didn't seem to need much crying time. After a few minutes he emerged. He went into the bathroom, splashed some water on his face and came out. Tracey followed him down the stairs.

He went directly to the front door. His grandfather was in the living room and he bellowed, 'Where do you think you're going?'

Martin didn't reply. He left the house, and Tracey left with him. He wasn't dragging his feet this time. He was walking as if he had a purpose, some place to go. Even while invisible, Tracey could feel her heartbeat quicken. Was this it? Was Martin on his way to meet their enemies?

They were coming to a playground and this appeared to be Martin's destination. Tracey looked around, wondering if she'd spot Serena, Clare, or any of the people she and other Gifted students had encountered in the past. But all she saw was the kind of people one would expect to find in a playground – some little kids with parents over by the see-saw and swings, and a group of teenage boys on the basketball court.

The latter group was the one Martin approached. He planted himself on the court just in front of the boy who held the ball. Like the other guys in the group, the player looked to be around sixteen or so. All the boys were bigger than Martin.

'What do you want?' the boy holding the ball asked.

'I want to play with you guys,' Martin said.

Oh no, Tracey thought. She didn't have to be Emily to see what the immediate future held for Martin. The boy would tell him no. Beat it, kid. Get lost, jerk. Something like that. Martin would refuse, maybe try to take the ball. The other guys would jeer. And Martin's inner superhero – or in his case, supermonster – would come out.

But the older boy just shrugged. 'Sure. I need another guy on my team. Go take a position over there.'

Was she crazy, or was that disappointment she was seeing in Martin's eyes? He scowled.

'Forget it,' he muttered, and walked off the court.

His next stop was a picnic table just a few yards away where a group of men were playing cards. A couple of them looked kind of rough and there was a bottle of cheap whisky on the table. Tracey got nervous.

Martin tapped one man on the shoulder. 'I want to join your game.'

A grizzled face turned to him. 'You play poker, kid? Sure, take a seat.'

Once again, Martin's face fell. 'Never mind.' And he walked away.

Now Tracey understood. Martin didn't want to play basketball or poker. He wanted to be teased, taunted, brushed aside. He wanted those older boys who played basketball, the men at the poker table, to mock him, make fun of him, laugh at him. Then his so-called 'gift' would be summoned. Martin had been looking for a way to be strong, to assert himself in the only way he knew how.

But then why did he resist the gift when it started to emerge in his back yard? OK, maybe he didn't want to hurt a blood relative. This was interesting, she mused. It meant that Martin actually had some control of his gift – it seemed like he could stop his gift from taking him over, but he still couldn't make it happen by himself – she knew how frustrating that must be for him because she was having a similar problem. It also meant he had feelings, that he wasn't just this whiny wimp who didn't care about anyone but himself. So there might be more to Martin than any of his classmates ever suspected.

But as she walked alongside him while he dragged himself slowly home, she was pretty sure that whatever else Martin might be, he wasn't a spy.

Chapter Four

I N MOST OF HER classes, Jenna sat at the back of the room, where she wouldn't be noticed and the teacher would be less likely to call on her. If she became bored – and this happened frequently – she could amuse herself by reading the minds of her classmates. Outside the Gifted class, she could benefit from the fact that no one knew what she could do, and no one could block her. In her last class, she'd been nicely entertained by a student's memory of a family trip to New York City.

But this was her English class, one of the few classes where Jenna sat closer to the front and paid attention. She'd always been a book person, and in this class, they'd been given some good stuff to read. And Ms Day, the teacher, had a way of getting the students to talk about the literature they'd been assigned. Right now, they were reading *Jane Eyre*, and even though the language was old-fashioned, Jenna liked the heroine. For someone who'd had a crummy childhood, Jane was actually a pretty gutsy girl, and Jenna could relate to her. She was looking forward to discussing chapter four today.

But it was not to be. On this Tuesday, Ms Day was absent, and a substitute was taking her place. Mr Roth was a frequent substitute at Meadowbrook, and Jenna slumped back in her seat when she saw him at Ms Day's desk. It was always the same when Roth took over a class. Jenna prepared herself for fifty minutes of utter boredom.

First, the substitute glanced at the lesson-plan book. 'You're supposed to discuss chapter four of *Jane Eyre* today. Let's see . . .' he looked at the roster. 'Johnson, Alex. Summarize chapter four.'

A boy responded. 'Uh, I didn't get a chance to read it.'

Roth scowled. 'Kitchens, Laurie. You summarize chapter four.'

A girl squirmed in her seat. 'Um, I *did* start reading it last night, but I – I fell asleep before I could finish it.'

Jenna, who rarely volunteered in class, was almost ready to raise her hand and offer a summary, but Mr Roth had apparently already given up.

'Well, you can't discuss it if you haven't read it. So, you can all use this class time to read chapter four.'

The girl sitting next to Jenna raised her hand. 'What if we've already read it?'

'Then read it again,' Roth stated. 'Or read chapter five.' With that, he opened his briefcase, took out a newspaper and unfolded it.

Students used the unexpected free time for a variety of purposes. Industrious ones started homework assignments. One girl began filing her nails, while a couple of boys put their heads on their desks and closed their eyes. Jenna had no desire to attack homework or sleep, so she scanned the minds of selected classmates for something interesting to entertain her.

. . . I'll go to Gametown after school and see if the new Infernal Toxic Battleground Warriors game is in yet . . .

. . . I wish I had my iPod . . .

. . . Jane Eyre is boring. Why can't we ever read anything good? Something with vampires . . .

Jenna uttered a silent groan. There wasn't anyone in this class worth spying on . . .

But that brief thought led her to something actually worth contemplating – the spy in the Gifted class. Someone was taking the information learned in the class and passing it on. How else would people like Serena, Clare and Stuart Kelley know so much about them?

It had to be Amanda. Everyone else could be eliminated for one reason or another. Emily and Tracey were completely out of the question, of course. It couldn't be Ken – if he could feel guilty about ignoring the voices in his head, he wasn't the type to betray his classmates. And according to what Tracey had told them at lunch today, the guilty party wasn't Martin.

Sarah . . .? Maybe all that niceness was just a mask. No, Jenna couldn't suspect Sarah. She might make fun of Sarah, calling her Miss Perfect or something like that, but deep down she instinctively knew that Sarah was a genuinely good person. There was a bit of mystery to her, that was true, but it seemed to be something personal and private. She wouldn't do anything that would hurt anyone else.

They could forget about Carter – he couldn't even communicate. For a brief time, when she first entered the class, she'd toyed with the notion that Carter's oblivious attitude was an act. But once, when Charles had one of his tantrums and sent books flying off shelves, everyone else in the class had covered their heads. Carter hadn't even flinched until Madame had instructed him to duck. No, the guy was truly out of it.

What about Charles? He could be pretty nasty . . . but she remembered how he'd helped her and Ken rescue the kidnapped students. Someone in cahoots with the bad guys wouldn't have done that.

No, it had to be Amanda. Before she came to the Gifted class, none of them had been threatened by outside forces. Amanda had no real friends in the class so she had no sense of loyalty to anyone. Tracey had said she thought there was some sort of romantic connection between Amanda and Ken, but from the way Ken talked about Amanda now, any friendship they might have had was finished.

And now Amanda had chosen to work in Mr Jackson's office.

Jenna had always harboured uncomfortable feelings about Mr Jackson, and not just because he was the school principal. There was something about him that gave her the creeps.

Madame had assured the class that no one else at Meadowbrook knew about them. The administration thought the students in Madame's class had some unusual aspects to their personalities or learning skills, and that was why they'd been brought together for a class under her supervision. None of them, not even the principal, was aware of what they could do. Jackson knew they had 'gifts', but he thought they were little personality quirks and talents. Not weird supernatural stuff.

And yet, the way Mr Jackson looked at them . . . Surely he suspected something. It was Jackson who brought Serena to their class as a student teacher. It was Jackson who had accepted the man who called himself Stuart Kelley as Jenna's father. Jenna had no difficulty picturing the principal and Amanda working together to exploit the gifted students.

The Gifted class met right after this class. That meant Amanda should be working in the office right now.

The one good thing about substitute teachers was the fact that they were more gullible than real teachers. Jenna got up and went to the desk.

Mr Roth looked up from his newspaper with annoyance at being interrupted. 'Yes?' he asked testily.

'I need to go to the clinic,' Jenna said.

His eyes narrowed with suspicion. Jenna elaborated.

'I think I'm going to throw up.'

That comment set Roth in motion. Frantically, he grabbed an excuse pass from the top drawer and practically threw it at her.

Once out in the hall, Jenna knew she needed to work out another story right away. It wasn't like she could walk into the office and just hang out. She needed a reason for being there. But what possible excuse could she have for going to the office? She could claim that Mr Roth sent her for some classroom supplies . . . but then she'd be handed the supplies and sent back to class. She needed to stay in the office for a while so she could observe Amanda and figure out what she was up to. This was not going to be easy . . .

But she was in luck. There was a lot going on in the office when she arrived, and she didn't have to provide an excuse, at least not right away. A counsellor with a red face was demanding to see Mr Jackson immediately. The custodian was complaining about something nasty in a bathroom, while two teachers were arguing over the use of some video equipment. And a couple of boys who'd obviously been in some sort of fight (and who wanted very much to continue fighting) were being held apart by another teacher.

Ms Simmons, the head secretary, was yelling at them all, telling them to sit and wait until Mr Jackson could see them. Amanda was behind the desk, in front of a computer screen, and not paying any attention to what was going on.

Jenna approached cautiously and tried to get a better look at what Amanda was doing without letting Amanda get a glimpse of her. She couldn't see what was on the screen but she could get into Amanda's mind, which was even better. There, Jenna could not only get a vague image of the screen, but she could also get a sense of how Amanda was responding to what she saw.

Amanda was looking at an email inbox. Her own? No, not unless Amanda normally received emails with subjects like 'Budget request for physical education equipment' and 'Board of Education Meeting Schedule'. It had to be Jackson's email. And if Amanda had access to the email account of the principal, wasn't that an indication that they were pretty chummy?

Now she needed to know what Amanda was thinking about the emails she was reading . . .

'Hello, Jenna, what are you up to?' Mr Gonzalez, the counsellor she saw regularly, was standing there. 'Not in any trouble, I hope!' He said this with a broad smile, showing that he was just teasing her.

Jenna forced a smile, but it wasn't easy, because Mr Gonzalez had a booming voice and she knew Amanda must have heard him. She didn't even have to look at her classmate to confirm this. Her connection to Amanda's mind had been severed.

At that moment, Mr Jackson came out of his office. 'Who's next?' he called out. Several of the office occupants clamoured for his attention, and Jenna decided to take advantage of the moment to explore the principal's thoughts.

But as hard as she tried, she couldn't penetrate his mind. Then she was aware of Mr Jackson staring straight at her and there was a flash of something in his expression that she couldn't interpret.

'What are *you* doing here?' he demanded to know.

Jenna looked around for an excuse. 'Uh, Mr Roth needs a stapler.'

Jackson took one off the desk. 'Here.'

Jenna took the stapler from him. 'Thank you,' she said, hoping she sounded polite and casual, but her stomach was suddenly in knots. There was something about the way Jackson was looking at her . . .

Hurrying out, she tried to dismiss this sudden sense of apprehension that had come over her. Why hadn't she been able to get even a glimpse of the principal's thoughts? And why had he glared at her like that? It wasn't like he could know she'd been trying to read his mind.

Unless . . . unless he knew what Jenna was capable of doing, and he'd blocked her. He'd know because Amanda had told him. Which was precisely the kind of thing a spy would do.

Back in the English class, Mr Roth was still reading his newspaper and the students were still doing whatever they'd been doing when she left. Jenna took her seat, stuck the stapler in her backpack, and opened *Jane Eyre*.

Much as she liked the story, it was hard to concentrate. Her thoughts kept going back to the scene in the office. Now she was more convinced than ever about Amanda. She couldn't wait to get into the Gifted class and share her news with Emily, Tracey and Ken.

But there was nothing she could do right now, and there were still thirty minutes of this class left to go. She plunged back into *Jane Eyre*.

The story grabbed her this time, and soon she was completely absorbed in it. The next time she glanced at the clock, she was surprised and pleased to see there were only about five minutes left before the bell would ring. But as it turned out, she didn't even have to wait that long to leave the room.

The door opened, and Amanda walked in. With an air of importance, she strode briskly up to Mr Roth and murmured something to him. The teacher looked at the class.

'Jenna Kelley?'

Jenna looked up. 'Yes?'

'You're wanted in the office.'

Jenna frowned, and looked at Amanda, but Amanda's expression didn't give her any hint as to why she was being summoned. She picked up her backpack, stopped at the desk and retrieved another hall pass, and left the room. Amanda was right behind her.

'What's going on?' Jenna asked her.

'Not a clue,' Amanda replied. 'Ms Simmons told me to come and get you. I just follow orders.'

I'll bet you do, Jenna thought sourly. They walked along in silence for a moment. At the end of the corridor, however, Amanda turned right instead of left, which was the direction to the office.

'I don't have to go back to the office,' she offered by way of explanation. 'Mr Jackson said I could go on to my next class.'

Jenna doubted that Amanda was actually going to appear early for the Gifted class. She'd undoubtedly use this time to go into a bathroom where she could fuss with her hair and her make-up and admire her own reflection for as long as possible. Jenna had once read a biography of a famous female spy named Mata Hari. *She* paid a lot of attention to her appearance too. Maybe it was a female spy thing.

As she approached the office, the reason for her summons dawned on her. The stapler she'd borrowed – Ms Simmons wanted it back. She took it out of her backpack, and when she entered the office she held it out to the secretary.

But Ms Simmons barely glanced at the stapler. Her disapproving eyes were on Jenna herself, and Jenna thought the secretary looked just a little too harsh considering the situation. So she'd kept the stapler for half an hour – big deal.

Ms Simmons nodded towards Mr Jackson's closed door. 'You're wanted in there,' she told Jenna.

Jenna's forehead creased in puzzlement. Now what? But Ms Simmons offered no further explanation. Jenna crossed the reception area and rapped on the principal's door.

'Come in,' the principal called.

Jenna opened the door. And then she just stood there, her hand still on the doorknob. It was an unexpected and unsettling scene that greeted her.

Mr Jackson sat at his usual place, behind his massive desk. On the chair facing him sat Jenna's mother. By his side stood a uniformed police officer. Jenna wasn't sure who looked more frightening – the cop with his stern expression, or her mother, who had tears in her eyes.

'Oh Jenna,' her mother moaned. 'Why did you do this?' She couldn't seem to bring herself to even look at Jenna as she spoke.

Jenna stared at her in utter bewilderment. 'Why did I do what?'

Mr Jackson had no problem looking at Jenna. 'You know our policy about weapons,' he said.

'No,' Jenna replied honestly.

'It's in the student guide,' the principal snapped.

Yeah, like anyone ever reads *that*, Jenna thought, but she decided it would be wiser not to say it out loud.

'We have a "no-tolerance" policy,' the principal continued. 'Do you understand what that means?'

Jenna nodded slowly. 'I guess it means nobody should bring any kind of weapon to school, right?'

'That's right,' Mr Jackson said. 'It doesn't matter if it's an assault rifle or a sling-shot.' He opened his drawer. 'Or a knife.'

It was a big, sharp knife, the kind that Jenna

imagined would be used for carving meat. Jenna stared at it blankly.

'Where did that come from?'

'Your locker.' He placed the knife down on the centre of his desk. 'Unfortunately for you, we held a random locker search today.'

An odd, shivery sensation went up her spine. 'I – I've never seen that knife before in my life.'

'Of course you haven't,' Mr Jackson said with a sneer. 'It just sprouted legs and walked into your locker. It even knew your combination.'

Jenna turned to her mother. 'Mom, I swear, it's not mine! I didn't bring a knife to school.'

'I want to believe you, Jenna . . .' her mother began, and her voice broke.

Mr Jackson finished the sentence for her. 'But she can't, because we have the evidence. I'm sorry, young lady, but you're in serious trouble.'

'Are you suspending me?' Jenna asked.

'Given your history, I don't feel suspension is an adequate punishment,' the principal declared. 'You are being sent back to Harmony House, for an indefinite period.'

Jenna froze. She opened her mouth to protest but no words came out.

And she wasn't only mute. She had difficulty hearing too. Vaguely, she was aware of being told that the police officer would escort her to Harmony House, but the sound seemed to be coming from very far away. Her mother was saying something too, but the words made no sense at all. Maybe because she was crying as she spoke.

Then she was in the hallway, with the policeman's hand on her shoulder. The bell must have just rung, because there were people in the hall, and she knew they were looking at her. Strangely enough, she wasn't upset, she wasn't humiliated. She didn't care. How could she?

She'd gone completely numb. She was too shocked to feel anything at all.

Chapter Five

TRACEY WAS IN THE bathroom when three girls she didn't know made a noisy entrance. They were talking loudly and excitedly.

'I saw it all!' one of them told the others. 'Police officers took her away! Five or six of them! And she was in handcuffs!'

'No way!' another one exclaimed.

'Really, I swear!'

'What did she do?' the third girl asked.

'I don't know but it's serious. They don't call the police for cutting a class.'

Uneasily, Tracey turned to the group. 'Who are you talking about?'

'You've seen her around,' the girl told her. 'She's that goth girl. I think her name's Jeannie or Janie, something like that.'

'Jenna,' Tracey said. 'Jenna Kelley.' She slung her backpack over her shoulder and left the bathroom.

In shock, she managed to get up the stairs without tripping. This had to be a mistake. Maybe the girl in the restroom hadn't understood what she saw. Or maybe there was another goth girl at Meadowbrook. She told herself that when she walked into Room 209, Jenna would be there, just as she always was. She even concocted a story that would account for what the girl in the bathroom had seen: a police officer had been invited to speak in Jenna's last class and Jenna was simply escorting him to the door. There had to be a reasonable explanation . . .

But when she walked into class, her heart sank. Emily's woebegone expression said it all.

'Do you know about Jenna?' Emily asked her.

Tracey sank into her seat. 'I heard people talking. They said she was arrested. Is it true?'

'It's something like that,' Emily acknowledged. 'I know a policeman took her away. I don't know what she did, Tracey, but it has to have been something really bad.'

'But maybe, maybe it wasn't because of something *she* did,' Tracey said. She thought frantically. 'Maybe . . .

maybe her mother was in an accident, and the police came to take her to the hospital.'

'There's nothing wrong with Jenna's mother.'

Tracey and Emily turned to see Amanda sauntering into the room. 'How do you know?' Emily asked.

'Because she was in Mr Jackson's office. First she came, then the policeman came, and then Ms Simmons sent me to get Jenna out of class.' Amanda sat down and whipped out her make-up bag.

'But *why*?' Tracey wanted to know. 'What happened?'

Amanda examined her own reflection in a little compact mirror. 'Well, Mr Jackson did a locker check today. He might have found something in Tracey's locker.'

'Like what?' Charles asked. 'Drugs? Guns?'

'I don't know,' Amanda replied as she applied lip-gloss.

Ken's eyes narrowed. 'Are you sure about that?'

Amanda snapped the compact shut. 'Just because I work in the office doesn't mean I know everything that goes on in there. All I know is that Mr Jackson suddenly decided to do some random locker searches and when he came back, he wanted to see Jenna.'

'It was a knife,' Sarah said softly.

Everyone turned in her direction. 'How do you know?' Tracey asked her.

'I saw it,' Sarah said. 'I'd just been excused from class to get some water. Mr Jackson and a policeman were in the hallway. Mr Jackson opened a locker and took out a big knife. I didn't know whose locker it was.' She shook her head sadly. 'I can't believe Jenna would bring a weapon to school.'

'Why not?' Amanda asked. 'I mean, she was a juvenile delinquent, right?'

Emily looked stricken. 'That's not true!' She amended that. 'OK, maybe it was a little bit true, but she's not like that now. You don't know anything about her, Amanda.'

'I know all I want to know,' Amanda murmured. She took her mobile phone out of her bag and began composing a text message.

'You reporting on this to someone?' Ken asked her.

Amanda looked at him. '*What?*'

But then Madame walked in. Everyone turned to her expectantly.

'Madame, did you hear about Jenna?' Emily asked.

The teacher nodded. 'I don't have all the facts. I've been told that something unacceptable was found in her locker during a routine security search.'

'Was she suspended?' Tracey asked.

'I believe so,' Madame replied. 'As I said, I don't have all the facts yet.' Tracey knew Madame had to be upset about this. But being Madame, her tone was calm and unemotional.

'I know we're all upset, but we can't jump to conclusions. Try not to listen to any gossip you might hear. And I don't think we should discuss this in class until we know more about the situation. Today, I suggest we spend the class time practising our relaxation techniques.'

As usual, Martin and Charles groaned, but Tracey could see the point of this. The exercises – in breathing and meditation – were supposed to help them control their gifts. Today, the soft music and Madame's soothing voice would help calm their feelings.

But even as they went through the motions of the exercises, Tracey's mind continued to race.

She knew all about Jenna's past, how she used to

practically live on the streets. Anything was better than staying at home with an alcoholic mother who used the apartment as 'party central' for her drinking buddies. Jenna hung out in train stations and bus stations, with people who wouldn't be considered good citizens. Pickpockets, druggies, people with actual criminal records . . . they weren't exactly Jenna's friends, but they accepted her as another troubled soul with nothing to do and no place to go.

Tracey knew Jenna herself had never been violent, and she never took drugs or did anything illegal. But she liked to act tough, she hung around with tough people, and she had got into trouble because of them.

But that was then, and this was now. Jenna's life had changed dramatically. She had a home with a sober mother, she had friends, she no longer saw her old street gang. She wasn't looking to get into trouble, and there was absolutely no reason for her to bring a knife to school.

So why did Mr Jackson find a knife in Jenna's locker?

Ken thought he knew. The second they were dismissed, he motioned for Emily and Tracey to join him in the hallway.

'It's a set-up,' he declared. 'Jenna didn't bring a knife to school. Someone put a knife in Jenna's locker.'

'But why would anyone do something like that?' Emily asked in bewilderment.

'To get rid of her,' Ken said. 'And I know who that someone is.' He looked past the girls. They both turned to see Amanda sweep by them.

Ken waited until Amanda was beyond hearing before he spoke again. 'I've got it all figured out. Amanda knows Jenna thinks she's the class spy.'

Tracey broke in. 'How could Amanda know that? Jenna never accused her.'

'She didn't have to, not out loud,' Ken said. 'Haven't you seen the dirty looks Jenna's been giving Amanda?'

Jenna gives lots of people dirty looks, Tracey thought. But maybe Ken had noticed something she hadn't.

'Besides, maybe Jenna *did* say something to Amanda,' Ken continued. 'Anyway, Amanda had to get Jenna out of her way. So she plants the knife, she sends Mr

Jackson an anonymous note telling him that Jenna's got weapons, and Jenna's suspended.'

Emily gazed at him thoughtfully. 'Ken, have you been reading a lot of detective novels lately?'

Ken ignored that. 'Think about it – it all makes sense. Working in the office, Amanda could get her hands on Jenna's locker combination. And it would be easy for her to slip a note under Jackson's door when no one was looking.'

Tracey had to admit there was logic in what he said. But . . .

'You can't prove this, Ken, can you?' she asked.

'Maybe I won't have to,' he said. 'If we can get her to confess.'

'How can we get her to do that?' Emily wanted to know.

Ken smiled grimly. 'I've got a plan. What means more to Amanda than anything else?'

Tracey blanched. Surely Ken wasn't suggesting that they threaten to destroy the contents of Amanda's closet.

But Emily understood. 'Her reputation. Being cool.'

Now Tracey got it. 'Right, she has to be the queen bee, everyone's supposed to look up to her.'

'Especially her pals,' Emily added. 'What did Jenna call them? The Evilettes.'

'Exactly,' Ken said. He glanced at his watch. 'I'll bet she's still at her locker – that's where she meets her friends after school. C'mon, let's go.'

On the way there, he explained his plan. Personally, Tracey thought it sounded a little cruel, and it certainly wasn't going to be easy for them to pull it off. But if it could bring Jenna back, she supposed it was worth a try.

As Ken suspected, Amanda was still at her locker, with two of her friends, Nina and Katie. Amanda was tapping her foot impatiently.

'Where's Britney?' Tracey heard her say as they approached. 'We're going to be late for our manicures.'

'Hey, Amanda,' Ken called out. Emily and Tracey said nothing, but it didn't matter. The three girls only had eyes for the boy. Even though Ken was no longer a top athlete at Meadowbrook, his good looks and general popularity still made him a catch.

'Hi, Ken,' they chorused with identical flirty smiles on their faces.

He focused on Amanda. 'Listen, Amanda, I have to tell you something.'

She cocked her head coyly. 'What?'

'Martin's got a thing for you.'

Her forehead puckered. 'Who?'

'Martin Cooper, from our class. Jenna read his mind yesterday, and she told me it came through loud and clear. He likes you. She meant to tell you today, but like, you know, she didn't get a chance. Anyway, I thought I'd pass it on.'

Nina giggled. 'Martin Cooper? That little wimp?'

And Amanda rolled her eyes. 'What makes you think that I would care if Martin Cooper likes me?'

Now Ken's face reflected confusion. 'But – but you told me, remember? You said you kind of liked him. So I thought you'd want to know that the feeling is mutual.'

Amanda's mouth dropped. 'I never said anything like that!'

'Oh, was it supposed to be a secret?' Ken asked. 'Sorry.' With that, he turned away and started towards the door. Tracey and Emily followed. But Tracey couldn't resist turning round to get a glimpse of Amanda's reaction.

The girl looked positively shocked. But what was even more interesting were the faces of her friends. They were both staring at Amanda as if they'd just learned she had a contagious disease.

CHAPTER SIX

THE LOBBY OF HARMONY House hadn't changed since the last time that Jenna had seen it. The same puke-green walls, the same row of orange plastic chairs, the same stupid poster that proclaimed: 'Today is the first day of the rest of your life.' The other people in the lobby might not have been the same ones who were waiting the last time she was here, but they fell into the same categories. Angry boys, sullen girls, unhappy parents, bored social workers . . .

Jenna sat on one of the orange chairs and stared at the poster. If the rest of her life was going to be like today . . .

The policeman sitting next to her interrupted her thoughts.

'Looks like it's going to be a while.'

Jenna said nothing.

'By the way,' the officer said, 'my name is Jack. Jack Fisher.'

What was she supposed to say now? He already knew *her* name. And 'pleased to meet you' didn't seem exactly appropriate, under the circumstances.

'You've been here before,' he said.

Jenna didn't look at him as she responded. 'How did you know?'

'I've read your file,' he said. 'I was kind of surprised . . .'

This time she actually glanced at him. 'About what?'

'You didn't seem like a repeat offender. Actually, it didn't seem like you committed much of an offence to begin with. They didn't find any drugs on you, did they?'

Because I wasn't doing any drugs, Jenna answered silently. But her response to the cop was simply a shrug.

'In fact,' he continued, 'it sounded to me like your biggest crime was being at the wrong place at the wrong time, with the wrong people. Am I right?'

Again, she only shrugged.

'I talked to your counsellor at school, that Mr Gonzalez,' the cop remarked. 'He said you've been doing pretty well at Meadowbrook since you started there.'

This time she didn't even bother to shrug.

'So what happened?' he asked. 'Why did you have that knife?'

Jenna couldn't hold back any longer. 'What do you want me to say, that I was framed?' she asked. 'That someone set me up? Isn't that what all the criminals say?'

Jack Fisher didn't blink. 'Sometimes it's true.'

It wasn't what she'd expected to hear from him, and for a moment, she was tempted to say more. But what if she came right out and accused Amanda Beeson? What good would that do? Amanda, who came from a 'good' family, who was one of the most popular girls at school, versus Jenna Kelley, who lived in a public housing estate, with no father, a recovering-alcoholic mother – a girl with a 'file'. Who'd come out on top?

But even though Amanda was superficial and selfish and full of herself, it was hard to believe that she could be this downright evil. Then again, if she was spying on their class and working with serious bad guys, it made sense.

Still, it had come as a complete shock, that scene in Jackson's office. Her mother . . . she'd been so upset. Would this incident make her start drinking again?

She could feel tears forming in her eyes. She needed to brush them away, but she didn't want to call attention to herself.

But Jack Fisher was watching her. 'Are you feeling sorry about something?' he asked softly.

Jenna turned to him and spoke fiercely. 'I've got nothing to be sorry for.' She clenched her fists. If there was anything worse than a regular cop, it was a cop who pretended to care.

A voice from the other end of the lobby called out, 'Jenna Kelley?' Jenna rose.

'Would you like me to come with you?' the cop asked.

Jenna shook her head. 'I know the routine.' She turned her back on Jack Fisher, but he touched her shoulder.

'I'm the police liaison for Harmony House,' he told her. 'So I'll be seeing you.'

It was on the tip of her tongue to reply, 'Not if I see you first,' but all she managed was, 'Whatever.' And she took off for the registration ordeal.

Entering the office, she saw that prissy white-haired Ms Landers was still the so-called director, sitting behind a desk. The woman gave her a sad smile.

'I wish I could say it's nice to see you again, Jenna.'

Jenna slumped into the seat facing her. She knew what was coming next – the 'welcome to Harmony House' speech, which was supposed to assure you that this wasn't a prison; to consider your stay here as an opportunity to search your heart and soul; to come to an understanding of why you're here; to exorcise bad habits; to explore other ways of expressing yourself; blah, blah, blah. It was all crap, of course. The prisoners were called 'residents,' not inmates, and there were 'resident assistants' instead of wardens, but there were bars on the windows and guards stationed at the doors. They called Harmony House a rehabilitation centre, but it was no better than a prison.

After the speech came the rules, and those hadn't changed either. The demerit system – any infraction of the rules would result in demerits, issued by the resident assistants. The accumulation of demerits would result in the loss of privileges.

Girls were confined to one side of the building, boys to the other, and the only interaction would talk place at mealtimes or in the TV lounge or at scheduled 'activities'. Jenna recalled a compulsory 'disco night' and shuddered. No phone calls or visitors the first forty-eight hours, which was fine with Jenna – she wasn't feeling very sociable.

When the director finally finished her speech, Jenna thought she'd be released to go to her room, but she'd forgotten another Harmony House ritual.

'Now, you'll see Doctor Paley for your intake interview,' Landers informed her.

There hadn't been a 'Dr Paley' the last time she was here. It had been a Dr Colby then. But now that she'd been reminded of it, Jenna knew what was coming.

Dr Paley was a smiling, plump, bald man in a white coat.

'Hello, Jenna,' he said jovially. Jenna grunted in return. Dr Paley didn't seem dismayed – she figured he probably never got much more than a grunt from the young people he dealt with here.

With a nurse by his side, he listened to Jenna's heart, took her pulse and blood pressure, looked in her ears and down her throat – all the usual stuff. Everything must have checked out OK, because he kept smiling.

When he finished, he told the nurse that she could leave, and invited Jenna to take a seat across from him at his desk.

'Let's have a little chat,' he said, opening a folder, which Jenna presumed was her file. Jenna didn't bother to stifle her groan. The last time she'd been here the doctor had only been interested in her physical state. This was something new.

'You're a shrink,' she muttered.

His perpetual smile broadened. 'Well, I'm a medical doctor who specializes in mental as well as physical health. I provide therapy for the residents here.'

'There's nothing mentally wrong with me,' Jenna declared. 'I'm not crazy.'

'You don't have to be crazy to benefit from therapy,' the doctor said. 'You've been sent here, to Harmony House, which indicates that you have some problems that need to be examined and resolved. I believe the best way to deal with problems like yours is to talk about them.'

Yeah, like you have any idea what my real problems are, Jenna thought bitterly.

The questions started.

'How's life at home, Jenna?'

'Fine.'

'I see that your mother's been through a rehabilitation programme. How do you feel about that?'

'Fine.'

'And I see you started a new school recently. How is that going for you?'

'Fine.'

'Have you made friends there?'

'Fine . . . I mean, yes.'

He turned a page in her file. 'I see you're taking geometry, English, geography . . .' he paused. 'What's this "gifted" class?'

Jenna sat up straighter. 'It's just this little special class for kids who are . . . gifted.'

'Gifted in what way?'

Jenna tried not to squirm. 'Different ways.'

'What's your gift? Are you a computer genius? Do you play a musical instrument?'

'No. It's not that kind of a gift.' She knew he wouldn't be satisfied with that, so she tried to remember what she'd once heard Tracey tell someone. 'Actually, I don't know why they call it "gifted". Each student has something – something sort of unusual going on. Like one guy, he's in a wheelchair. And there's another guy who used to be a big athlete, but he had an accident and he can't play sports any more.'

The doctor nodded. 'And what's unusual about you?'

'I'm a juvenile delinquent.'

'I see . . .' He eyed Jenna keenly. He wasn't smiling now. 'I'd like to hear more about this class.'

Jenna shifted in her chair. 'I'm kind of tired.'

The smile returned. 'Of course – you should go to your room and get settled. We'll talk another time.'

Finally, she was released. When she left the doctor's office, a woman with a tag identifying her as a 'resident assistant' escorted her to her room on the second floor.

'You're lucky,' the woman told her. 'We're not

completely booked right now so you don't have a roommate.'

That was a major relief. The last time Jenna had been here, she'd been stuck in a room with a twelve-year-old shoplifter who cried incessantly. Jenna thought she was incredibly stupid – what good would crying do in a place like this? If you were stuck here, you just had to grit your teeth and get through it. She'd tried to be a good role model for the girl, acting tough and invulnerable, but the girl never seemed to pick up on Jenna's example. At least this time she wouldn't have to put up with anyone's tears.

The room looked just like the room she'd had the last time. Twin beds, a white dresser, two desks. The only difference was the picture on the wall. In the last room, she'd had a cutesy picture of puppies. This time, she had kittens.

She threw herself on one of the beds and stared up at the ceiling. Now what? She had no computer, no TV, no music . . . She remembered that there was a little library downstairs, by the dining hall. She could go and check out a book.

But there was no time for that now. A bell rang,

signalling dinner time. Jenna had no appetite, but she knew she had to show up for the meal. It was one of the rules. She still didn't know how long she'd have to stay here, but she had no intention of extending the time by breaking any of the rules.

In the dining hall, she picked up her tray and went to an empty table. Unfortunately, it didn't stay empty. A girl who looked a little younger than she was joined her.

'Can I sit here?'

Jenna shrugged. Her shoulders were definitely getting a workout today.

The girl sat down. 'I haven't seen you around before,' she said. 'Is this your first day here?'

Jenna nodded.

'It's not so bad,' the girl said. 'I mean, I was really scared at first. Some of the kids are *mean*, you know? Like, they've done violent things. All I did was break into a car with some friends and take it for a ride. We didn't hurt anyone.'

Jenna gritted her teeth. Oh no, this one was a talker. She had to get rid of her.

'What did you do?' the girl asked.

'They found a knife in my locker at school,' Jenna said.

'A penknife?'

Jenna shook her head. 'No, a great big butcher's knife.'

'What were you going to do with it?'

Jenna met her eyes. 'Cut up some people who were getting on my nerves.' While she spoke, she fingered the cutlery on the table. The 'knife' was a plastic thing, and couldn't do any damage, but the girl got the hint.

Alone again, Jenna pushed the food around the plate and kept an eye on the clock. In twenty minutes she'd be allowed to leave. She set her expression in a scowl that she hoped would keep all potential tablemates away.

A guy ambled towards her. With his zits and his sandy hair pulled back in a ponytail, he looked young, but not young enough to be one of the inmates. When he got closer, she saw that he had on one of those 'resident assistant' tags.

'You Jenna Kelley?' he asked.

She deepened her scowl. 'Who wants to know?'

He smirked. 'Peter Blake, resident assistant.' He indicated his badge. 'Can't you read?'

Jenna glared at him. 'What do you want?'

'Just to say "hi", welcome to Harmony House.' He pulled out a chair and sat down. 'What are ya in for?'

Jenna considered possible responses, and settled on, 'Weapons.'

Peter nodded, and Jenna could have sworn he almost seemed impressed. He probably thought she was referring to guns. Well, let him think what he wanted to think.

His next question was unexpected. 'You got friends?'

'Yeah, why?'

'They can't visit for forty-eight hours,' he told her.

'I know that. I've been here before.'

His eyebrows went up. 'Oh, yeah? Then you probably know the game. How things work here. Demerits, privileges . . .'

'I know the rules,' she said shortly.

He grinned. 'Sure you do. After a couple of days, you can have visitors. I'll bet you've got cool friends.'

'Yeah, they're OK,' Jenna acknowledged. What was he getting at?

'Are they cool enough to do you some favours?'

Still puzzled, Jenna asked, 'What kind of favours?'

'Oh, come on,' he said, 'I thought you knew the game.'

'What game are you talking about?'

Peter Blake rolled his eyes in exasperation. 'Your friends do favours for you. You do favours for me. I return the favour.'

'I don't know what you're talking about,' Jenna declared.

He grinned. 'You will. I just want to know if you're going to play along.'

Jenna still didn't understand what he was suggesting, but she was pretty certain it wasn't something on Harmony House's list of rules and regulations.

'I'm not playing at anything,' she said flatly. 'I don't owe you any favours and I don't want any from you.'

He raised his eyebrows. 'Yeah? Well, don't say you weren't warned.' He got up. 'See ya around.'

Weirdo, Jenna thought. What did he want, assault

rifles? And what would she get in return – extra helpings of dessert? What a jerk.

But at least he'd helped her pass the time. She could leave the dining hall now.

She stopped at the little library to find something to read, and she was almost pleased to find a copy of *Jane Eyre*. It was funny, in a way. One of the only advantages of being sent here was the fact that she wouldn't have any homework assignments. Actually, she would *get* the assignments – the school would send them to Harmony House. But it wasn't like she had to do them – no one would be checking on her. And yet here she was, voluntarily taking on the task she'd be doing at home.

Back in her room, she settled down on the bed and opened the book. She'd read enough of the book to know that Jane had endured some pretty rough times in a boarding school that was like a jail. Now Jenna could identify with the character even more.

But it was hard to concentrate on reading. Her mind kept going back to the events of the day. Tracey and Emily – all the students must know by now what had happened to her. Madame too. What were they thinking of her?

And her poor mother, who was trying so hard to make up for the bad times. But here was her daughter, getting into trouble again.

Could she ever convince them that she'd never brought a knife to school? That the whole thing had been a set-up? That Jenna Kelley was not a committed criminal?

Over and over, she relived the scene in Jackson's office. Finally, she put the book down, turned over and buried her head in the pillow. It seemed she would have to put up with someone's tears after all.

Her own.

Chapter Seven

Waiting for the school bus on Friday morning, Tracey moved away from the other kids and took out her mobile phone.

'Hello?'

Tracey tried to sound natural. 'Hi, Amanda, it's Tracey!'

'What do you want *now*?'

Tracey couldn't blame her for sounding annoyed. This was the fourth time she'd called in three days. In the background, she heard another voice – Nina's, or maybe Britney's.

'Who is it?' And she heard Amanda respond, 'Nobody.' Tracey talked fast before Amanda could hit the hang-up button.

'I just wanted to remind you to save a seat for me at lunch. I'm planning to sit with you.'

'Stay away from me!' Amanda shrieked. And Tracey was disconnected.

Relieved that her morning obligation was finished, Tracey tossed the phone back in her bag. But she still had the lunchtime duty to do – and she wasn't looking forward to *that*.

It was one of Ken's ideas. Yesterday, Tracey had picked up her tray in the cafeteria and carried it over to the table where Amanda and her friends always ate lunch. Britney, Nina and Katie were already there, but Amanda hadn't arrived yet. The three Evilettes stared at her, as if an alien had just landed at their exclusive gathering place.

'Amanda invited me to join you guys,' Tracey had explained.

'She *did*?' Katie asked in disbelief.

'When?' Nina wanted to know.

'Oh, we were on the phone last night, for ages,' Tracey lied. 'We talk all the time, you know. Anyway, she said she wanted me to sit with you all from now on.'

Amanda arrived with another of her friends, Sophie. She was clearly taken aback to find Tracey at *her* table.

'What are you doing here?' she asked bluntly.

Nina answered for her. 'Tracey said you invited her.'

'I did no such thing!' Amanda exclaimed.

'Don't you remember?' Tracey asked. 'Last night, when we were talking on the phone, you said—'

Amanda didn't let her finish. 'I didn't talk to you on the phone last night! I've never called you in my life!'

Tracey had tried to look concerned. 'Are you OK, Amanda? Are you having memory problems?'

At that point, all the girls were looking at Amanda. Amanda was speechless.

Tracey spoke sadly. 'Are you ashamed of us being friends, Amanda?' Then she rose, picked up her tray, and walked away.

She had no idea what happened at the table after she left, but she suspected that it hadn't been too comfortable for Amanda. Today, Tracey planned to arrive at the table after Amanda, and she would thank Amanda for having called last night to apologize for her rude behaviour.

Ken had also given Emily jobs to do. Yesterday,

she'd passed a note to Nina in a class they had together.

Nina, if you see Amanda next period, could you tell her she can borrow my yellow sweater this weekend. She's been begging me to lend it to her.

Despite the fact that Tracey wasn't crazy about these efforts to destroy Amanda's reputation, she had to laugh at the notion of the well-dressed queen bee wanting to wear anything of Emily's.

The bus arrived. Tracey hurried to climb on so she could get a seat at the back, where the driver wouldn't see her on the phone. They weren't supposed to use their mobile phones on the bus, but if he couldn't see her she'd be OK. The passengers never told on each other.

She got her seat, and took her phone out again.

'Good morning. Harmony House.'

'Hello, can I speak to Jenna Kelley, please?'

'I'm sorry, Jenna can't come to the phone.'

Tracey frowned. This was the same response she'd been getting each time she tried to call her. 'Well, can you tell me when visiting hours are?'

'I'm sorry,' the voice on the other end said again, 'but Jenna isn't permitted visitors.'

'Why not?' Tracey demanded to know.

'Have a nice day,' the voice replied, and the line went dead.

This was too frustrating. Even prisoners in real jails were allowed to have visitors.

When she met Emily on the steps at Meadow-brook's entrance, she learned that Emily had been getting the same information from Harmony House.

'I can't believe that no one is allowed to have visitors in that place,' Tracey fumed.

'Maybe Jenna doesn't want visitors,' Emily suggested. 'You know how she doesn't like people to feel sorry for her.'

Ken was waiting for them just inside the building. He didn't bother with greetings.

'What did Amanda say when you called her this morning?' he asked Tracey.

'What she said when I called yesterday,' Tracey said. '"Leave me alone."' She sighed. 'Ken, how much longer do we have to do this? I hate going to that table at lunchtime. They don't want me there and I don't want to be there.'

'I'm going to try to get her alone this afternoon,' Ken said. 'I'm going to tell her we'll stop if she'll confess to what she did to Jenna.'

Emily was looking at Ken quizzically. 'Ken,' she began, and then she bit her lip.

'What?' he asked.

Emily hesitated. 'I don't know how to say this, and – and I know it's none of my business, but . . .' She looked at Tracey. Tracey had a feeling she knew what Emily was about to say and it was something Tracey had been wondering about herself.

'Go ahead,' she said.

Emily spoke carefully. 'I used to think . . . well, we all used to think that there was something going on between you and Amanda. Like, you were sort of interested in each other, you know what I mean?'

Ken didn't say anything.

Emily went on. 'But now . . . it's like you totally hate her.'

Ken shrugged. 'Sure, I hate what she did to Jenna. And the way she put us all in danger when she was involved in the seance.'

Tracey took over. 'Are you sure it's not something

97

else too? Like, maybe you're going overboard because you still have feelings for her.'

Ken glared at her. 'And maybe you're defending her because she took over your body and got you a nice haircut.' And he took off before she had a chance to deny it.

'I'm going to the bathroom before class,' Emily told Tracey. 'Want to come with me?'

Tracey shook her head. 'I want to find Madame. Maybe she can talk to those Harmony House people so we can visit Jenna. See ya in class.'

'I won't be there – I've got a dentist appointment,' Emily told her. 'I'll call you tonight.'

Tracey hurried upstairs to Room 209. Madame wasn't there, but someone else was.

The Queen of Mean, who could usually be found wherever she could see and be seen, and who was always surrounded by friends, was hidden away in an empty classroom and all alone. And she didn't look mean today. People who were truly mean didn't bury their faces in their hands.

'Amanda?' Tracey murmured.

Amanda looked up. Instantly, her expression

changed – but now she seemed more frightened than mean.

'Leave me alone!' she hissed. 'Stop bothering me!'

Tracey took the seat next to her. Ken had said he'd talk to Amanda later, but Tracey figured this was as good a time as any to hit her with the ultimatum.

'Look, Amanda, you can make us stop bugging you right now. All you have to do is come clean about Jenna.'

'What are you *talking* about? I didn't do anything to Jenna!'

She seemed honestly and sincerely bewildered. Ken would say that Amanda was putting on a good act, but Tracey wasn't so sure.

'We think you set up Jenna to get her into trouble. You work in the office, which means you can get your hands on the master key to the lockers.'

Amanda still looked confused. Tracey was going to have to spell it out to her.

'You put the knife in Jenna's locker.'

Amanda's eyes widened. 'Why would I do that?'

'Because . . . because she was on to you. And you wanted to get rid of her.'

Amanda didn't blink. 'On to me about *what*?'

Tracey took a deep breath. 'We think you're the spy, Amanda. We think you're the one who's communicating with our enemies: Serena, Clare – all those people who want to use us.'

Amanda gasped. 'Are you nuts? Why would I do something like that?'

'Because . . . because . . .' Tracey tried to think of a way to explain their suspicions which wouldn't be too hurtful. It was impossible, so she told the truth.

'Because you're selfish,' she said finally. 'You don't care about anyone – you only think of yourself. You think you're better than the rest of us.'

Amanda's eyes narrowed but she didn't deny any of the accusations.

'And you took that job in Mr Jackson's office so you can find out more about us,' Tracey finished.

Now Amanda became annoyed. 'Is that what you think?'

'Well, you don't need the job. And I seriously doubt you're interested in learning office skills. So what other reason could there be?'

Amanda's lips tightened. Tracey got the feeling there was something she wanted to say but she was keeping it inside.

'It's not just me,' Tracey added. 'Jenna, Emily, Ken . . . we all think you're spying on us.'

'Ken . . .' Amanda murmured. 'So that's why he's been acting so nasty.'

'That's why we've *all* been acting nasty,' Tracey corrected her, but she could tell it was only Ken that Amanda cared about.

'If he only knew why I took that job, he'd feel so bad about treating me like this,' Amanda declared hotly.

Tracey blinked. 'Then why don't you tell him? I mean, *us*? You could tell me right now why you took that job.'

For once, Amanda seemed uncertain. She bit her lip, and rapped her manicured fingernails on the desk. Finally, she spoke.

'Can you keep a secret?'

'That depends,' Tracey said carefully. She hated the idea of swearing to secrecy before she knew what the secret was. What if Amanda was up to something that might put all the Gifted students in danger?

'I'm not going to tell you unless you promise not to tell anyone,' Amanda stated. 'Not your friends, not Madame, not anyone.'

Tracey was torn, but she knew that if she didn't give in she'd learn nothing. 'OK, I promise. Why did you take the job in the principal's office?'

Despite the fact that they were alone in the classroom, Amanda lowered her voice.

'Remember when I went into the hospital last month to get my tonsils out?'

Tracey nodded.

'Well, you know that wasn't me in the hospital.'

Tracey nodded. 'Like I told you when you came to school, Emily and I went to visit you at the hospital. We could tell it wasn't you.'

'And you remember who I was when I was out of my body.'

Again, Tracey nodded. 'You were the woman who was working with Serena on that seance scam. I forget her name.'

'Margaret. And when I was in Margaret's body,

Serena took me to a meeting. And you know who else was there? Clare, the woman who kidnapped us. And that man who claimed he was Jenna's father.'

'So there really is a conspiracy,' Tracey murmured in wonderment.

'Someone else was there too,' Amanda said. She did another of her dramatic pauses.

'Who?' Tracey asked impatiently.

'Mr Jackson.'

Tracey drew in her breath sharply. Nobody liked Mr Jackson, and Jenna was always saying he gave her the creeps. But this was a little hard to believe.

'But Madame says he doesn't know about us!' Tracey exclaimed.

'Madame doesn't know everything,' Amanda countered. 'I'm pretty sure it was Mr Jackson who planted the knife in Jenna's locker.'

'But – why?'

'If he's in on the conspiracy, then he knows about Jenna's gift,' Amanda said. 'Jenna was in the office earlier today, and Mr Jackson saw her. Maybe he was thinking about us, and he was afraid Jenna read his mind. So he had to get rid of her. I can't prove it, but he did leave the office just after Jenna was there, even though there were all these people waiting to see him.'

'Maybe he had to go to the bathroom,' Tracey offered weakly.

Amanda gave her a sceptical look. 'Yeah, sure. And maybe he went to the cafeteria and picked up a knife.'

Tracey's head was spinning. But everything Amanda said made perfectly good sense.

'What did Madame say when you told her about Mr Jackson?' Tracey wanted to know.

'I didn't tell her,' Amanda replied. 'And you're not going to tell her either.'

'But Amanda, this is important! If our own principal is working against us, we're in danger right here at school!'

Amanda agreed. 'And I'm going to prove it. All by myself. That's why I'm working in the office – so I can watch him, so I can listen in on his meetings and phone calls, and read his emails. I want to get real evidence.'

'But you've already got evidence,' Tracey protested. 'Even if you can't prove that he put the knife in Jenna's locker, you know he's guilty of *something*. You saw him with your own eyes. Well, Margaret's eyes. He was meeting with people who have tried to get to us. That proves he's a bad guy.'

'It's not enough,' Amanda said. 'Who's going to believe that I was in someone else's body?'

'Madame would.'

Amanda shook her head. 'That's not enough. Look, Tracey. You said I think I'm better than the rest of you. Well, socially, that's true. I am.'

Tracey rolled her eyes. 'You're not exactly modest, Amanda.'

Amanda ignored that. 'But you guys look down on me! You think my gift is worthless, you think I can't do anything important. Well, I'm going to show you I can.'

So *that* was what this was all about. It wasn't enough for Amanda to be the prettiest, the best-dressed, the most popular girl at Meadowbrook. She wanted to be queen of the Gifted class too.

'Amanda, that's stupid!' Tracey declared. 'We should all be working together on this.'

'And let someone else get the credit? Forget it!' Amanda began ticking items off on her fingers. 'It was

Jenna who figured out that Serena was hypnotizing Emily to get winning lottery numbers. Ken saved Jenna from going off with that man who said he was her father. Charles got the gun away from Clare in the bank robbery. *You* pulled the scarves off Serena at the seance. Well, now it's *my* turn to be the hero.'

'But this is too dangerous!' Tracey protested.

Amanda looked at her watch. 'The bell's about to ring.' She got up. 'So now you know I'm not the spy, and you'll stop hassling me, right?'

'But how am I going to persuade the others to stop if I can't tell them what you're up to?'

'Find the real spy,' Amanda said. She started out of the room, but paused at the door and looked back. 'Did you say you visited me at the hospital?'

Tracey nodded. 'With Emily.'

Amanda frowned. 'Did anyone see you there? Were any of my real friends visiting?'

'Not while we were in the room.'

'That's a relief,' Amanda said, and left.

Tracey didn't even feel insulted – by now, she was used to the way Amanda protected her social reputation. Besides, she was still reeling from Amanda's revelation and she couldn't give much thought to anything else.

Mr Jackson, their very own principal! He wasn't exactly loved by the students, but he was an important man in a highly respected position. He was an educator! How could someone like that be a criminal?

She supposed it was possible that Amanda had just made up the story, to throw suspicion off herself. But Tracey didn't think so. Amanda just didn't seem like she had that much imagination. And it *was* Mr Jackson who had brought Serena into their class . . .

It was all beginning to make sense. If they were in on this together since the beginning, Serena would have told Jackson what she'd learned about their gifts. But Serena wasn't around any more, and someone was still feeding Jackson information. Someone in the class.

But if Amanda wasn't the spy, then who was? There was still one person she considered to be capable of treachery – Charles. Now was as good a time as ever to check out *his* private life. So, just before the Gifted class, she ducked into the bathroom.

Taking a deep breath, she closed her eyes and conjured up an image of her former self, friendless and lonely. She dredged up sad memories of isolation, alienation, feeling worthless and unimportant. She concentrated intensely on the emotions she'd known back then and the sensation of not being seen. She visualized herself fading away, and then she started to feel it. The sensation of being weightless, lighter than air . . .

She opened her eyes and looked at the mirror over the sink. There was no reflection. She was getting better and better at this! Pleased with herself, she left the bathroom, went upstairs, and positioned herself outside Room 209, where she could hear what was going on.

There wasn't much to hear, though. Apparently, Madame had set them to work on some sort of writing assignment, and her classmates were industriously scribbling away in silence. So she amused herself by roaming around the building, dancing in front of oblivious hall monitors and peeking through classroom windows. She considered going to the office and checking out Mr Jackson's activities – but there was always the chance she might inadvertently reappear. She couldn't risk it.

She came back to Room 209 just before the bell rang. When the door opened, Charles was the first to emerge. That wasn't unusual – he could make that wheelchair go very fast, and the others stepped aside to let him pass. Tracey was never sure if that was because they were trying to be kind or if they were afraid he'd run them over. She suspected that Charles would prefer the latter reason.

Ken was right behind him. She thought she might tell him what she was up to. It was comforting to know he could hear her when she was invisible, when no one else could. But Ken brushed by her so quickly, she didn't have a chance, and Charles was moving in the opposite direction.

People jumped out of the way as his motorized chair tore down the hall to the lift. As far as Tracey knew, he was the only student permitted to use it. She hopped in with him, and rode down to the main floor.

She'd never paid attention to how Charles got home. Today, for the first time, she noticed the white van parked just in front of the exit. A man stood by the vehicle, and when Charles appeared, he opened the back door. A ramp slid out, and the man pushed

Charles's chair up into the van. Tracey stayed close behind, and got inside just before the man closed the door.

It wasn't until the van pulled away that she got a look at Charles's face. It was red, and she wondered why. Was it from the exertion he'd expended, hurrying out of school? Or maybe he was embarrassed by the van and the assistance he'd needed to get into it.

Funny how she'd never thought about how Charles might feel, being unable to walk. She didn't even know how the situation came to be – if he'd been in an accident or something like that. It dawned on her that she'd never had any sort of private conversation with Charles. She didn't think anyone in the Gifted class knew much about him. She doubted that anyone had ever been invited to his home.

It was a very nice house, all on one level but large, with a fine, freshly mowed lawn. At the end of the drive she saw a couple of bicycles leaning against the garage wall, and a basketball net hanging over the door. She remembered Madame saying something to Charles about having brothers. Hadn't Charles said that they were ashamed of him?

The man pushed Charles out of the van and started wheeling him up the drive. 'Beat it!' Charles growled. 'I can do it.' The man released him and Charles took control of his chair. But instead of continuing up the drive he turned the chair so it rolled over the grass, making ugly tracks on the lawn.

'Charles!' Tracey exclaimed, forgetting for a moment that he couldn't hear her. Not that it would have made Charles move back on to the drive. He had a tight smile on his face that made her think he was messing up the lawn on purpose.

The woman who opened the front door obviously thought so too.

'Charles!' she cried out. 'Stop that! Look what you're doing to the grass!'

Charles rolled himself up the ramp and right past her without a word of greeting or apology. Then he turned to the right, accelerated, and sped into what looked to Tracey like a very formal living room with a white carpet – over which there were now streaks of brown and green from the wheels of Charles's chair.

'Oh, Charles!' There was a note of resignation in the

woman's voice, which led Tracey to believe this wasn't the first time Charles had pulled a stunt like this.

Charles stopped in the middle of the room and looked at a fancy vase filled with flowers on a pedestal. The vase rose up, moved towards Charles, then fell and broke, sending flowers and shards of glass all over the floor.

'Charles, why are you doing this?' the woman wanted to know.

Charles ignored her. He crossed the room, raced down a long hallway and turned into a room. The door slammed shut before Tracey could reach it.

Astonished, she looked back at the woman to catch her reaction to this little performance. At first, she'd presumed this was Charles's mother, but now she realized she must be someone who worked here. Probably the person who would have to clean up the mess. She wondered what would happen when the woman reported Charles's behaviour to his parents.

She couldn't get into Charles's room now because he'd closed the door. The front door was still open though, so she went out to check if she could look into Charles's window and see what he was doing.

But something else distracted her. A couple of boys were now on the carport, shooting baskets. As she moved closer, she saw the family resemblance. Both boys had Charles's red curls and freckles. They were close in age, maybe fifteen and sixteen.

She wondered if they were both on the basketball team at the high school. Tracey didn't know much about basketball, but they looked like they played pretty well – most of their attempts sent the ball through the basket.

But then one of the boys threw the ball towards the basket and it veered off in another direction. The other boy grabbed the ball, tossed it, and it went straight up in the air, so high that it disappeared. Then it came down so fast both boys scampered away to avoid getting hit on the head by it.

They both looked annoyed, but not surprised. 'Charles!' one of them bellowed.

That was when Tracey noticed an open window, and Charles looking out of it.

'Charles, knock it off,' the taller boy called out.

'Make me!' Charles responded. To Tracey, he sounded like a five-year-old.

The other boy moved towards the window and spoke calmly. 'Why don't you come out and play with us?'

'Yeah, I'll run around and chase the ball like you,' Charles said sarcastically.

'You can play in your chair,' his brother said. 'You know there are whole teams who play basketball in wheelchairs. I've seen them on the Sports Channel.'

'If I can't play like a normal person, I don't want to play,' Charles replied.

The boy sighed. 'OK, don't play. But you don't have to mess up our game, OK?'

Charles uttered a word that would have sent him straight to Mr Jackson if he'd said it at school. The ball flew up from the ground and settled on the roof of the house.

'Thanks a lot, Charles,' one of the boys muttered. Charles's window slammed shut.

Maybe he'd be coming out of his room now, Tracey thought. As she started back towards the door, a car pulled into the drive. The boys got out of the way and the car went into the garage. A few seconds later, a nice-looking woman with a shopping bag in her hand emerged.

'Hey, Mom,' the boys called out to her.

'Need a hand?' one of them added.

'No thanks, dear, I can manage,' she said cheerfully. She paused and looked at the lawn. The cheerful expression vanished. 'Oh, no. Charles must be in one of his moods.'

The woman Tracey had seen earlier opened the door for the woman. 'I'm so sorry, Mrs Temple. I couldn't stop him. I'm cleaning the mess in the living room now.'

'I'll help you,' Charles's mother said.

Tracey skipped on ahead of her so she could get back inside the house. She was interested in seeing how Mrs Temple was going to deal with Charles's behaviour. Would he be grounded, lose privileges?

But Mrs Temple didn't even go to Charles's room. She disappeared for a few minutes, and when she returned she was carrying a vacuum cleaner. She joined the other woman in the living room.

This must be normal behaviour for Charles, Tracey realized. His mother was upset, but she didn't seem at all surprised by the mess he'd made.

She stood there, watching the women clean the

carpet and waiting for Charles to come out of his room. Suddenly, out of the blue, a dish came floating across the room. It carried a stack of cookies, and as it whizzed past her, cookies fell off and dropped on the carpet. Mrs Temple sighed, and put the vacuum cleaner down. Picking up cookies along the way, she kept pace with the plate. Tracey went too. When the plate reached Charles's door, it opened. Mrs Temple went in, and Tracey followed.

Charles was on his bed, watching TV. He barely glanced at his mother. He made the plate settle on his lap, took a cookie and crammed it into his mouth.

This was something new, Tracey realized. Charles had summoned the plate from another room that was not in his line of vision. She'd never before seen Charles move something without being able to see it. So his gift was evolving and changing too, like hers. But he hadn't shared this with the class.

'Charles, I want to talk to you,' his mother said.

Charles didn't respond. His mother took the remote control and switched off the TV. *That* got a response.

'Hey!'

For a moment, Tracey felt like she was watching a

replay of what had gone on in Martin's house. There was a big difference, though, between Martin's bullying grandfather and Charles's mother. Mrs Temple sat on the edge of her son's bed, and gazed down at him with serious concern.

'Charles, why do you do these things?' she asked him.

'What things?' he mumbled.

His mother's voice became sterner. 'Things like ruining the lawn, when you could have gone up the drive to the back door.'

'I just wanted to see what it felt like, to be on the lawn. I would have walked on it but I can't walk, in case you haven't noticed.'

'Why did you make the vase fall?'

'Because I wanted to smell the flowers. Only I couldn't because I can't stand up.'

She indicated the plate of cookies. 'You summoned your snack here, and now there are cookies all over the floor. Were you just too lazy to go to the kitchen for them?'

'I'm not lazy!'

'Then why did you use your gift?'

Charles pressed his lips together tightly, as if he was trying to keep the words from coming out. His mother waited, but when he still didn't respond to her question, she sighed and shook her head.

'I don't know what to do with you, Charles.'

He had an answer for that. 'Just leave me alone.'

Silently, Mrs Temple rose and left the room. Tracey remained. Was Charles like this all the time at home? she wondered. Or was this an especially bad day for him? She recalled the expression on his face when he saw his brothers playing basketball. Maybe that was what set off this wave of bad behaviour.

She couldn't be absolutely, positively sure, but she thought maybe she knew why Charles acted like this. He felt helpless, and he used his gift to feel powerful.

He wasn't helpless, of course. Being in a wheelchair might give him a disadvantage, but lots of people had disadvantages. Charles used his gift so he wouldn't have to deal with the fact that he couldn't walk. He was hung up on being helpless.

She could understand, because she'd given in to helplessness herself. She blamed her parents for ignoring her – but what had she done to help herself? She'd wallowed in self-pity. Amanda had shown her how to break out. And it wasn't just the clothes, the haircut, the make-up. It was learning to stand up for herself.

That was what Charles had to do – stand up. He couldn't do it physically, but it was Charles's attitude that kept him down, not his legs.

He wasn't the class spy. He was just another sad kid who wanted to be like everyone else. And she could help him. She couldn't take over his body like Amanda had taken over hers. But she could talk to him, she could be a friend, and maybe he'd open up to her. His family loved him, but they couldn't understand his needs. She could, because she'd been there.

She wanted to help him, and she had to do it *now*. When else would she be able to corner him alone like this? If she could make a real connection with him, maybe she could encourage him to connect with the Gifted class, open himself up to the group experience. She knew she couldn't appear right in front of him, so she dashed out of the room and out of the open front door.

Behind a bush where she knew she wasn't visible from the house, she closed her eyes and concentrated on becoming visible. She envisioned herself as real and solid, and commanded her body to reappear. When she felt nothing happen, she gritted her teeth and worked harder, concentrating, focusing, directing all her mental energies into becoming herself. She couldn't remember the process ever taking this much energy before.

Opening her eyes, she realized why. She was still invisible.

And she began to get nervous.

Chapter Eight

JENNA SANK INTO THE chair in the lounge and looked at the TV screen without even seeing what was on it. She supposed she could take advantage of the fact that for once she was alone in the lounge, and she could watch something she wanted to watch. But she wasn't in the mood for TV.

She wasn't in the mood for anything. It was 5 p.m. on a Friday afternoon, and she'd been at Harmony House for three days. What would she be doing if she wasn't here? Waiting for her mother to come home from work, and thinking about what they might have for dinner. Maybe throwing some things in a backpack for one of the regular Friday night sleepovers at Tracey's. Checking online to see if there were any good movies playing in town.

Instead, she was imprisoned in a facility for bad teenagers, and she wasn't bad. And right now, all the really bad teenagers were enjoying visits from friends and families, while she, Jenna Kelley, who had done absolutely nothing wrong, was all alone.

That Landers woman had said she couldn't have visitors or phone calls for the first forty-eight hours. Those forty-eight hours were over twenty-four hours ago, and she'd had neither a visitor nor a phone call.

Peter Blake, the creepy resident assistant, came into the lounge.

'It's visiting hours,' he announced.

'Yeah, I know,' Jenna muttered.

'Guess you didn't get any visitors,' he commented.

Jenna didn't think she needed to dignify that with an answer.

He turned to leave, but looked back at her from the door. His lips curved unpleasantly into a smile that was more like a sneer. 'I wonder why.'

So did Jenna. Not one visitor, yesterday or today. Not from her mother, not from Tracey or Emily. She'd harboured a faint hope that Madame might have come to visit her. OK, maybe she acted like she didn't give a damn what Madame thought about her, but deep in her heart she did trust the teacher, and she thought the teacher trusted her. But now she had to wonder if maybe Madame thought she belonged in this prison.

At first she was surprised by the lack of calls and visits – now she was depressed. Did they all believe she'd really come to school armed with a butcher's knife? Had they all abandoned her? Was her very own mother on the phone right now to Social Services telling them to keep her daughter for ever?

It hurt, bad. Even during the worst times of her life, when her mother was drinking and Jenna was basically living on the streets, she couldn't remember feeling so low. So alone.

This morning, she'd had another meeting with that doctor, Paley. He'd asked her if she was making friends here at Harmony House. She'd lied and said yes, just to get him off her back. It wasn't like she could tell him she'd read a few minds and realized there wasn't anyone here she wanted to make friends with. So many of them were like the people she'd known before, on the streets.

She didn't even have to read minds to know that some of them were just deadly dull. Every day, there were 'group' sessions she had to attend. Around ten residents gathered with a counsellor to talk. What they mostly did was complain and find other people to blame for their situations – usually a mother or a father. It was boring.

So she'd been hanging out by herself, eating alone, not making any effort to connect with anyone. She supposed there had to be some decent people here, but she just couldn't get up the energy to make the effort to find them.

She'd been almost glad when another resident assistant, Carrie, told her she was getting a roommate yesterday. But when the new girl, Kristy, arrived, Jenna could see right away that her life was only going to get worse.

She didn't look terrible – in fact, she was something of a goth herself, with dyed black hair and several prominent piercings. She even had tattoos, something Jenna hadn't got into yet. But the minute Carrie left them alone together in the bedroom, Kristy reached into her bag and pulled out a cigarette.

Jenna didn't want the new girl to think she was some sort of goody-goody, but once Kristy lit up the smell was too seriously disgusting.

'Um, I'm pretty sure that's against the rules,' she murmured. 'Not that I care about rules,' she added hastily, 'but someone's going to smell the smoke in the hall and you'll get into trouble.'

No sooner had the words left her mouth than there was a sharp rap at the door and Carrie entered.

'No smoking,' she declared, and pointed to the very visible sign of a cigarette with a big X over it on the wall. She took the cigarette from Kristy, and then, without even asking permission, she went into Kristy's bag. Removing the pack of cigarettes, she said, 'You're getting a demerit for that.'

'Like I care,' Kristy muttered, as soon as Carrie left. She then began to regale Jenna with her reasons for being at Harmony House. It seemed that Kristy had been part of a gang that was robbing convenience stores. She went on and on about how cool it was to hold a gun and scare the wits out of some guy behind the counter at two in the morning.

She didn't say if she'd ever actually used the gun, and Jenna suspected she hadn't, because Kristy seemed like the type who would brag about it if she'd shot someone. As her tales went on, Jenna wondered which was worse — someone who wept over her crimes or someone who boasted about them. The latter, she decided. Her former roommate at Harmony House may have got on her nerves, but this one was truly creepy.

Fortunately, her new roommate discovered that some old pals of hers were in residence at Harmony House, and she spent the rest of the evening in search of them. Kristy slept late and skipped breakfast that morning — which resulted in another demerit — and Jenna didn't even have to eat lunch with her today in the dining hall. Kristy spent her lunchtime at the table famous for hosting the most serious offenders.

But Jenna couldn't avoid her for ever, and she wasn't surprised when Kristy ambled into the lounge. Of course, she wouldn't have any visitors — she was still in her first forty-eight hours. Without even asking Jenna if she was watching whatever was currently showing on TV, Kristy picked up the remote control and started hitting channel buttons. Then she reached into her pocket and took out another pack of cigarettes.

As she lit up, Jenna spoke.

'There's a resident assistant around,' she warned Kristy.

Kristy glanced at her briefly. 'That Peter guy, right?'

Jenna nodded.

Kristy uttered a short laugh, and took another drag. Jenna wondered if the girl was really as tough – or as stupid – as she acted. With nothing else to do, she poked around Kristy's mind.

. . . hate this place . . . maybe it won't be so bad . . . can't make phone calls, that sucks . . . gotta figure out a way to get in touch with Pete . . . tell him to come on Monday and bring E . . .

E . . . she *could* be referring to a person whose first initial was E. But it was more likely she was talking about Ecstasy. Oh, great, Jenna thought. Cigarettes were bad enough. Now this idiot was going to try to get high in here.

The smell of the cigarette was making her nauseous. Another resident, a boy, came into the lounge, and Jenna looked at him hopefully. Maybe the smell would bother him too, and together they could get Kristy to put out the cigarette.

But the boy wasn't staying. 'You guys seen Peter?'

'He's around somewhere,' Kristy said.

The boy seemed a little nervous as he touched the pocket of his jeans. 'Well, if you see him, tell him I've got something for him.'

Puzzled, Jenna couldn't help wondering why the boy looked so uneasy, his eyes darting around the room. One quick sweep of his mind gave her the answer. He was carrying a bag of weed.

That was when it hit her. Peter Blake was using residents to get drugs. He was telling them to get their visitors to smuggle the junk into Harmony House. Maybe he was bribing them with extra privileges – like giving Kristy the right to smoke. Or it could be blackmail. He'd discover someone breaking a rule and make a deal – no demerit in return for a favour.

And this would explain why she, Jenna, had no visitors. She leaped up, went out into the hall and down the stairs to the office of Ms Landers.

'Hey, you can't just go in there!' the secretary exclaimed. But Jenna walked right past her and opened the door to the director's office.

The director wasn't alone. That cop, Jack Fisher,

was sitting on the other side of her desk. Landers looked up with annoyance written all over her face.

'Young lady, you do *not* barge into my office like that!'

Jenna ignored that. 'I want to know why I haven't had any visitors,' she demanded.

The woman's expression didn't change, but at least she answered her. 'I explained this when you entered. The accumulation of demerits results in the loss of privileges. Five demerits means no visitors or phone calls for twenty-four hours.'

Jenna's eyebrows went up. 'I have five demerits?'

'Six, I believe. Let's see . . .' she turned to her computer and hit a couple of keys. 'Sneaking over to the boys' dormitory wing. Picking fights. Smoking in your room.'

As she continued with her litany of fabricated violations, Jenna wanted to hit herself on the head for being so incredibly stupid. Peter had asked her if she had friends who would do 'favours'. She didn't know what he was talking about, but he'd assumed she was refusing to ask her friends to bring in drugs, or whatever else he asked residents to smuggle in for him. So he'd made up infractions for her and given her demerits. It was a punishment for not cooperating.

She should have figured this out that first day, in the dining hall. But what could she have done about it? There was no way she'd ask her friends to do something like that. Her friends couldn't do anything about it anyway! She tried to picture Emily looking around a bad neighbourhood for a drug dealer.

'If you feel these demerits are unwarranted, you may appeal against them,' the woman said. 'But not at this moment – I'm busy. You can make an appointment with the secretary.'

Jenna left, and passed the secretary without bothering to make an appointment. What good would it do? She couldn't tell Landers about Peter Blake. She wouldn't believe her. And if she directed Landers towards the others who were being threatened or bribed, they'd only deny it. And how would she prove she was telling the truth? Admit to having read their minds?

Outside the office, she paused in the empty corridor and leaned against a wall to catch her emotional breath. She'd been screwed, that's all there was to it.

And there wasn't a damned thing she could do about it.

'Are you OK, Jenna?'

She hadn't even heard Jack-the-cop come out of the office.

'I'm fine,' she said shortly.

He reached in his pocket and pulled out a pack of chewing gum. 'Want some gum?'

'No.'

She knew how rude she must sound, but what did it matter? He'd heard Landers's report on her. He knew she was nothing but trouble.

But she could have sworn she saw something else in his eyes. And just out of curiosity, she peeked into his head.

. . . surprised . . . she doesn't seem like the type . . . is she covering for someone? Wish I could get her to open up to me . . .

She must have been staring at him, because he cocked his head to one side and smiled. 'Want to talk?'

She *did* – but not to him. Not to a cop. She didn't care how much sympathy she saw in his eyes or read in his mind, she couldn't trust him.

'No,' she said, and walked away. But just as she was about to turn the corner, she looked back at him. Somehow, she managed to get one more word out.

'Thanks.'

Chapter Nine

I N THE KITCHEN AT home, Tracey sat on the counter – a position that was forbidden in the Devon home. But it didn't matter, since her mother couldn't see her.

Her mother stood just a few feet away, with the phone in her hand.

'Tracey isn't here, Emily,' she was saying. She laughed nervously. 'Actually, she might very well be here, but she's not available, if you know what I mean. I haven't seen her since she left for school yesterday.'

There was a pause, which Tracey assumed meant that Emily was responding. Then her mother spoke again.

'No, I'm not worried. Not *yet*. I mean, this has happened before. I'm sure she'll turn up eventually.'

Eventually. That was the key word. Tracey hadn't gone this long without reappearing since – since the days before Amanda changed her. At least now her parents actually noticed that she wasn't visible. That was definitely an improvement.

Her problem now was figuring out how to share what she'd learned from Amanda yesterday. The only person she'd be able to communicate with was Ken. But every time she'd tried to defend Amanda, everyone told her she was being silly. They all thought that just because Amanda had inhabited Tracey's body and improved Tracey's life, Tracey had some dumb notion that she owed Amanda something.

But there was one other possible connection – Jenna. Could Jenna read the mind of an invisible person? Jenna could read people's minds when she couldn't see them, but Tracey couldn't recall any circumstance when Jenna had read her mind when she was invisible. Maybe if Tracey *thought* about what she'd learned from Amanda, Jenna would 'hear' her. Their gifts were constantly developing, evolving – she'd seen Charles display an aspect to his gift she'd never seen before. It was possible that her own gift, and Jenna's too, had potential they hadn't yet discovered.

But only if Jenna knew that Tracey wanted her

mind to be read. Tracey had to get close enough to Jenna to give her some kind of signal, to let her know. And how could she get close to her when she wasn't permitted any visitors?

Tracey had to laugh at herself. What an idiot she was! She was invisible, she didn't need anyone's permission to visit Jenna.

She had to take three buses to get to Harmony House, but her biggest problem was not the distance or the time it would take to get there. Her chief concern was getting on and off each bus; if no one else was waiting at the bus stop or getting off there, the bus wouldn't stop or open its doors. Fortunately, this only happened once, and someone came along, which enabled her to get on the next one. The positive aspect was the fact that she didn't have to pay for the ride – but being a basically honest person, she didn't feel very good about this. Riding for free seemed like stealing. But she couldn't waste energy feeling guilty about it – she had no other option.

Jenna's residence didn't look like a prison. The brick building was painted white, and it was set way back on a green lawn. The sign on the lawn read

'Harmony House,' not 'Detention Centre' or anything like that. There were bars on the windows, but they'd been painted white too and shaped in a design that made them look more like window decorations. Tracey suspected that the two men who were standing on either side of the front door were guards, but at least they weren't dressed like guards, and she couldn't see any guns. They could have been doormen at a hotel.

When someone came out, she slipped inside. Now the place looked more like an institution, with its sickly green walls and the lobby that seemed more like a waiting room. But Tracey had no time to waste on criticizing the decor. She had no idea if she might suddenly become visible again. This was a pretty big place and she had no idea where Jenna might be.

Luckily, it was dinner time, and she followed people who all seemed to be heading in the same direction – a dining hall. And there she found Jenna, sitting alone at a table.

From a distance, Tracey studied her friend, and her heart ached for Jenna. She wore that dark, angry face that Tracey remembered from when she first saw her, the day Jenna entered the Gifted class. Her expression had softened considerably since then. Even when Jenna was doing her 'I'm-tough-as-nails' thing, she didn't look so – so enraged. And something else too. Sad. In Tracey's opinion, sad was worse than angry.

She moved closer and closer, until she was at the table, standing right in front of Jenna.

Jenna, it's me, Tracey.

But Jenna's expression didn't change. Tracey wasn't surprised. If Jenna didn't know she was there, she wouldn't try to read Tracey's mind. How could she let Jenna know of her presence? She considered various possibilities.

Recalling her mother and the handbag, Tracey took a salt shaker from another table and placed it in front of Jenna. But the sudden appearance of a salt shaker didn't grab Jenna's attention. Obviously, her mind was elsewhere.

Tracey removed her own headband from her hair. It was something she wore a lot, and maybe Jenna would recognize it. She dropped it, and it landed right on top of Jenna's sandwich.

Jenna saw it, but her reaction wasn't what Tracey expected. She snatched up the band and stood up.

'Whoever threw this at me, you're in trouble!' she yelled.

A couple of kids giggled, but the people sitting closest to Jenna just stared at her blankly. Jenna walked over to the trash bins and dropped the headband in one.

Tracey watched her mournfully. It had been one of her favourites. But she should have known that Jenna wouldn't notice what other people wore, not even her closest friends. Jenna was the opposite of Amanda – she didn't care about stuff like that.

She'd probably know what she herself was wearing, though. Jenna's necklace, a thick silver thing with a dangling pendant of a skull, was one she wore frequently. Moving around the table, Tracey quickly lifted the necklace over Jenna's head and dropped it in front of her.

Jenna whirled around. But no one could have approached her and got away so quickly. She picked up the necklace and examined the clasp. Then she shrugged and put it back around her neck.

What else could she do, Tracey wondered. Gather up plates and bowls and dump them on Jenna's table? That would get Jenna's attention, but it would attract attention from the others in the dining hall too. She was getting desperate – she *had* to talk to Jenna. She had to share this information, she wanted Jenna's advice and opinion. Jenna would know what Tracey should do. She had to make contact with her. She needed her friend!

Suddenly, Jenna's eyes widened. 'Tracey?' she whispered.

Yes! Yes, it's me, I'm right across the table from you. How did you know I was here?

Jenna put a hand over her mouth and spoke so softly that Tracey had to lean across the table to hear her.

'I don't know, but it happened once before, when Emily was trapped by Serena at school. I guess she was trying so hard to make contact with me that I actually heard her.'

Just like me, Tracey said with feeling. *I've got to talk to you.*

'What's going on?' She'd taken her hand away from her mouth, and a couple of kids at the next table glanced at her curiously. Jenna quickly speared a carrot from her plate, stuck it in her mouth and chewed furiously.

Just listen. I've learned something. This wouldn't be breaking the promise she'd made to Amanda. Because she wasn't 'telling' the secret – she was only thinking it.

Silently, Tracey recalled the story Amanda had told her about Mr Jackson. *She's telling the truth, Jenna, I'm sure of it. And it all makes sense, when you think about it. The spy is reporting to Mr Jackson. That's how he found out about our gifts.*

'So it was Jackson who put the knife in my locker?'

I think so.

'But who's the spy?' Jenna asked. 'Who's telling Jackson about us?' Realizing she was talking out loud, she clapped a hand over her mouth but it was too late. People turned to look at her. And one guy, with a bad complexion and a ponytail, sauntered over to her.

'Talking to yourself, Jenna?' he asked unpleasantly.

Jenna glared at him. 'Does that get me another demerit?'

'No,' the guy said. 'Just a report to Doctor Paley.'

Can we go someplace private? Tracey asked.

Jenna rose, and picked up her tray. Tracey followed

her as she left the tray by the bins, and went out of the dining hall.

'We're going to my room,' Jenna murmured as they walked.

But they weren't going to get any privacy there. A girl was lying on one of the twin beds, and smoking a cigarette.

Jenna spoke. 'Get out of here with that cigarette or I'll ram it down your throat.'

The girl smirked. 'Is that a threat?'

'No,' Jenna said. 'It's a promise.'

Tracey was impressed. She knew Jenna could act tough, but she'd never heard her sound quite so scary.

The girl got the message. Once she was out of the room, Jenna threw herself on the other twin bed. 'That threat's going to get me another demerit. Which will probably mean another day of no visitors.'

Is that why they've been telling us you can't have visitors? Because you've got demerits?

Jenna nodded. 'Only I didn't earn them.'

Tracey was shocked to hear the story about the assistant who was blackmailing residents. *Can't you tell someone about him?*

'He'll only deny it. And how am I going to explain why I know about all the other kids he's using?'

But this has to stop! He'll keep making up stories about you, you'll get more demerits, and, and . . .

Jenna finished the thought for her. 'And I'll never get out of here.'

Just as she'd never heard Jenna sound as fierce as she had moments earlier, she'd never heard her sound so flat and resigned. She preferred the fierce Jenna. Maybe now Jenna needed Tracey as a friend even more than Tracey needed Jenna.

That's not going to happen. I'll get the proof we need, I'll get you out of here. I promise, Jenna.

There was a knock on the door, and then it opened. A young woman poked her head in.

'It's time for your group session, Jenna.'

Jenna groaned. 'Can't I skip it today?'

'Sure,' the woman said, 'if you don't mind getting another demerit. Oh, and Doctor Paley wants to see you tomorrow.'

'I just saw him this morning!' Jenna exclaimed.

The woman shrugged. 'Well, he wants to see you again tomorrow.'

'Boy, Peter works fast,' Jenna murmured.

The woman's brow furrowed. 'What do you mean?'

'Nothing.' Jenna got up and went to the door. Tracey followed her.

You want me to stick around?

Jenna shook her head. The woman looked at her curiously. 'Are you all right, Jenna?'

Jenna almost smiled. 'No. But I will be.'

Yes, Tracey thought fervently. *Yes, you will, Jenna.*

Outside Harmony House, she went to wait at the bus stop. Looking back at the building, she had the same thought she'd had when she arrived.

No, it didn't look like a prison. But a place didn't have to look like a prison to be a prison. A prison didn't even have to be a place. A secret was like a prison – it could keep a person trapped in the same way. Jenna, Tracey, Emily . . . all of Madame's students were imprisoned by their secret gifts.

Somehow, Tracey was going to get Jenna out of Harmony House. She'd find the real spy, and the spy would lead her to the proof about Mr Jackson and the knife. Jenna would be released, she'd be free. But could any of them ever feel completely, really and truly free,

free to do whatever they wanted, free to be themselves?

No one else came to wait at the bus stop, and the bus was approaching. Tracey could only hope that someone was getting off at this stop so she could get on. No, she wasn't free to do whatever she wanted.

Chapter Ten

WHEN TRACEY ARRIVED HOME, she could hear the Devon Seven and her mother in the kitchen.

'Where's Tracey, Mommy?' one of them asked. Tracey was pretty sure it was Brandie. The others chimed in.

'Where is she?'

'I want Tracey to play with us!'

'We can't find her, Mommy!'

Mrs Devon looked frazzled. 'She's – she's out, girls, she's busy. Go outside and play, Tracey's coming home soon.'

As soon as the kitchen was vacant, the woman sank down into a chair. 'Tracey?' she called out weakly. 'Are you in here?'

Her mother looked really upset.

'Tracey . . . I'm sure you're fine, you're just being

invisible, but . . . I'm worried! What if you're hurt? Maybe you've run away from home . . .' She gasped as another thought must have occurred to her. 'Maybe you've been kidnapped! Oh Tracey, sweetheart, if you're here . . . I know I wouldn't be able to hear you if you speak, and I know you can't write me a message, but . . . could you just give me a sign, so I know you're all right? You're not usually invisible for this long.'

Once again, Tracey marvelled at the irony of it all. Not so long ago she could have disappeared for a lot longer than a couple of days and her mother wouldn't have even noticed. Now she was worried . . . Tracey wasn't sure which feeling was stronger, her pity for her mother or her satisfaction at the change in family relationships.

It was the pity that made her go back into the living room, pick up her mother's handbag from the coffee table, and bring it into the kitchen. When the bag appeared in front of her mother, Tracey was rewarded with a sigh and smile of gratitude.

'Thank you, dear,' her mother said humbly. Tracey left and went up to her room. She had some thinking to do before she made her next move to fulfil her promise to Jenna.

OK, so Jackson was the major bad guy at Meadow-brook, the numero uno villain. But how was he getting his information about the gifted students? Someone was telling him what went on in class.

Tracey refused to even consider the notion that Madame would betray her students. The teacher was beyond any suspicion, and she was sure her classmates would agree with her. So it had to be one of them. From what she knew, and what she'd observed, she could eliminate herself, Jenna, Emily, Amanda, Sarah, Ken, Martin and Charles. Which only left Carter.

But how could Carter be a spy? The boy didn't speak, he didn't write, he couldn't communicate at all. He was practically a zombie.

She searched her memory for what she knew about him. Supposedly, he was found wandering on Carter Street. He carried no identification and the police had no reports of any missing boy who fitted his description. Social Services had taken over his care and he'd been placed in a foster home. That was all she knew.

From her desk drawer, she retrieved the Meadowbrook Middle School Directory, and looked up his name. The foster family was called Granger, and they lived not too far from her own home.

The address turned out to be a medium-sized, very ordinary looking cottage-style house on a tree-lined street. The sun was setting and the lights were on inside. She waited on the front steps for a while, but no one came in or out. Fortunately, the curtains weren't drawn, so she walked around the house and peeked in at each window.

She found Carter in what was clearly the dining room of the house. He was sitting at a table with two other young boys, a man and a woman. She assumed the adults were the Grangers. The two younger boys didn't look at all alike, nor did they look like the adults, so she thought they might be foster children too.

The Grangers certainly fed their foster kids well. The table was laden with food – roast beef, bowls of vegetables, a big tossed salad. She couldn't hear any conversation, but she could see lips moving as the family talked. It seemed to her that they were having a lively conversation. Of course, Carter wasn't partici-pating in it. He ate, slowly and rhythmically, but he stared straight ahead, not making eye contact with anyone else at the table. It was the same way he behaved at school. She saw the woman bend over and speak to him, but Carter didn't respond.

It dawned on her that she was hungry. Eating while invisible wasn't easy. Even if she could get herself inside the house without anyone noticing a door opening, she couldn't very well join them for their meal. There were too many people at the table and someone was bound to notice if food started to disappear.

So she stood there, suffering hunger pangs, and waited for the meal to end. Only, what did she expect to happen after that? The boys would probably watch a little television and go to bed. There wouldn't be much to see through the windows. She had to find a way to get inside the house and into Carter's room. Maybe there she'd find something interesting about Carter, some clue as to whether or not Carter had a secret life as a spy.

Fortunately, when dinner was over and the table was being cleared, she observed the woman saying something to Carter again. He got up and left the dining room. Skipping over to the next window,

Tracey could see him scraping leftovers from the plates into the trash bin in the kitchen. Then he took out the garbage-packed liner and went to the back door.

Tracey hurried to position herself by the back door and as soon as Carter opened it she slipped inside. While Carter took the garbage to the outdoor bin, she did a quick survey of the kitchen. A platter of leftover roast beef slices hadn't been put away yet.

A benefit of being invisible meant she didn't have to think about manners. She snatched up a slice of meat and practically crammed the whole piece in her mouth. Then she took a second slice. Mrs Granger came in and picked up the platter. Looking at the remains of the meat, her brow furrowed for a minute, as if she'd realized there was less there than she thought there should be. Finally, she shrugged and wrapped the slices.

Carter returned.

'Could you help me load the dishwasher, Carter?' the woman asked.

Carter didn't say yes or no, but he opened the door of the dishwasher and began loading items. He was just like he was at school, obeying without communicating.

Tracey left the kitchen and went down a hall which she presumed would lead to bedrooms. One bedroom held a big double bed, and she assumed that was the master bedroom. Another bedroom had bunk beds and toys strewn on the floor.

She decided that the third bedroom must be Carter's. It held one single bed, a desk, a bureau and a bookshelf. Everything was impeccably neat and tidy.

With no one else in there, she had the freedom to open drawers. All she found there were clothes. Desk drawers contained pencils, a ruler, ordinary school stuff. She couldn't find any notes or letters.

Next, she checked the books on the shelves. She tried to remember if she'd ever seen Carter reading, but no image came to mind. Actually, the books all looked pretty new and untouched. She opened a few in the half-hearted hope she might find a note tucked inside, but she had no luck.

It was frustrating. There had to be something in this room but she couldn't tear it apart and make a mess. She'd have to wait until Carter came in and hope he would reveal something to her. To pass the time, she took one of the books from the shelf, a biography of

Helen Keller. Maybe the Grangers had given it to him in the hope that he might find something in common with a person who overcame disabilities. She sat at Carter's desk, and started to read.

Once she sat down, she realized how exhausted she was. It had been a long day. The life of Helen Keller was intriguing but Tracey was too tired to get caught up in it. She put her head on the desk and closed her eyes.

It was amazing how easily she fell asleep in such an uncomfortable position. When she opened her eyes the room was completely dark. Rising from the chair, she saw Carter in bed, sound asleep.

The whole house was silent – everyone must be asleep, she thought. The bedside clock told her it was midnight. Well, at least she could get out without anyone seeing a door open by itself. She just hoped there was no alarm system.

Suddenly, making barely a sound, Carter sat up in bed. For a second, Tracey thought he was looking straight at her and that maybe she'd become visible. A glance at the mirror over the bureau told her that this hadn't happened.

Carter got out of bed and gathered up the clothes he'd been wearing earlier. Politely, Tracey averted her eyes while he dressed. He then walked out of the room.

Was he sleepwalking? Tracey wondered. She followed him down the hall and into the living room. Silently, he opened the front door.

On the street in front of the house, a black car was waiting. A man stepped out from the driver's side, and without speaking, he opened the back door. Carter got in, with Tracey close behind.

The driver took off. He said nothing to Carter and he seemed to know where he was going. The ride took about twenty minutes and brought them to a residential area on the other side of town. The car pulled up in front of a house on a tree-lined street. Again, the driver got out and opened the door.

Carter walked to the front door. Tracey hung back for a moment, to get a good look at the house so she could identify it later. It was white, smaller than Charles's home, but well kept and nice looking.

She'd expected Carter to knock or ring a bell but someone must have seen him approach from inside.

The door opened and Carter went in. Tracey raced forward but she was too late – the door had closed by the time she reached it.

Furious at herself, she raced around the house, looking for another way to get inside. There was a back door, but it was locked.

So she was in the same position she'd been in back at Carter's home, and she was forced to do what she'd done there – look for a window that would give her a view of what was going on inside. Again, the people were in the dining room and sitting around a dining room table. But they weren't eating.

She could identify all of them. Clare, the woman who'd been in charge of the bank robbery. Serena, the fake student teacher and medium. The man who called himself Stuart Kelley and claimed to be Jenna's father. And Mr Jackson.

Carter was offered the chair at the head of the table. Serena seemed to be talking to him – at least, she was looking at him and her lips were moving. And then Tracey saw something she'd never seen before.

Carter's lips were moving. With the window closed, Tracey couldn't hear anything, but it was obvious that

Carter was speaking. And whatever he was saying had the full attention of the others.

Clare was taking notes. Mr Jackson was nodding. Stuart Kelley appeared to interrupt at some point to ask a question. Carter responded.

At first, Tracey was stunned. Then, when she recovered from her surprise, she was furious. That weasel, that little fake – he was pretending to be a zombie and all the time he was perfectly capable of communicating. He must have an incredible memory too. She'd never seen him write anything down in class, but he was obviously able to remember everything he heard there so he could report to this evil gang. At least, that's what Tracey assumed he was doing – telling the others what went on in the Gifted class. But what else could intrigue this band of conspirators?

If only she could read lips! What was Carter telling them? How were they going to use the information?

Oh, how she wished *she* could communicate right then and there. She'd call her classmates, she'd call Madame at home, she wouldn't care if she woke them all up. She'd tell them where she was, they could join her, and together they could confront these people.

She couldn't tell them, of course. She wasn't physically capable of doing that. But maybe she could *show* them. From her bag, she drew out her mobile phone. In the menu, she clicked on the camera function.

The phone in her hand was invisible. Maybe any picture she took with an invisible camera wouldn't be seen. But she couldn't waste time pondering the logistics of invisibility. She manoeuvred the phone until she thought it was in the right position to catch the image of the table and the people around it, and clicked. In this darkness, it wouldn't be a great picture, and it wouldn't prove that Carter could talk.

But it would show that Mr Jackson was in league with those other villains. And that was a start.

Chapter Eleven

A T TEN O'CLOCK ON Saturday morning, Jenna found herself facing Dr Paley in his office. Behind the desk, the round-faced man gazed at her steadily. Jenna stared right back at him.

The doctor wasn't smiling quite as broadly this time. 'I don't usually come in to Harmony House on Saturdays,' he said. 'But I thought it was important to see you as soon as possible.'

Jenna affected a look of wide-eyed innocence. 'Why?'

'I think you know,' he said.

Of course she knew, but she wanted to hear it from him. She couldn't defend herself until she knew exactly what that creep Peter had said. So she simply shrugged.

Dr Paley gave in. 'When I checked my messages this morning, there was a new and urgent report about you. You've been observed talking to yourself.'

Jenna said nothing.

'And your expression indicated that you were listening to another voice. As if someone else was with you.'

Jenna remained silent.

'You don't deny it?' he asked.

Jenna chose her words carefully. 'I don't remember doing anything like that.'

Dr Paley looked at his notes. 'You appeared to be carrying on a conversation in the dining hall, and you were alone.'

Jenna shrugged. 'I was probably daydreaming.'

Dr Paley studied her thoughtfully. 'Who were you talking to, Jenna?'

What would he say if she replied 'my invisible friend'? The thought made her smile.

'This isn't a laughing matter,' he said.

Jenna shifted uncomfortably in her chair. 'Sorry. I guess I was just daydreaming again.'

'You don't strike me as a daydreamer,' he said. He looked at his notes again. 'I see you've amassed a lot of demerits. Smoking, picking fights . . .'

She tried to stop the fury from rising inside but it was impossible and she knew it came out in her voice. 'I've never smoked a cigarette in my life,' she declared hotly. 'And I haven't picked any fights. Not here, at least.'

'Then why do you have all these demerits?'

'It's all made up, I shouldn't have those demerits. Someone's out to get me.' And then she wanted to kick herself. Now he was going to think she was paranoid.

'Who's out to get you? Mrs Landers? Other kids?'

She shook her head.

He looked at the file. 'I see all these demerits were reported by the same resident assistant.'

She couldn't stop herself. 'Peter Blake.'

'Is that who's out to get you?' When she didn't reply, he asked, 'Why would he make up these things about you?'

'Because he's a slime bucket,' she muttered.

A brief smile flickered across the doctor's face. 'That may well be – I don't know the young man. But why would he pick on *you*?'

She was so sick of this, of beating around the bush, avoiding the questions. Of being Peter's victim.

'Because I wouldn't tell my friends to bring me drugs so I could slip them to him. He's punishing me by giving me demerits, thinking I'll give in eventually. And it's not just me.' She hesitated.

'Go on.'

'I'm not paranoid. That's what he does, you see. And if you do what he wants, he'll even look the other way if you break the rules.'

Dr Paley's bushy eyebrows shot up. 'He's doing this with other residents as well?'

She nodded.

'You've seen him do it?'

She hesitated. 'No, not exactly . . .'

'So they've talked to you about it? What do they say about it? Are they angry?'

'No one talks about it,' she told him, then realized her mistake.

'Then how do you know this is going on with people other than yourself?'

She had known all along that it would come down to this. She knew because she could read his mind, but there was no way she could explain that, and now she was just sounding paranoid. 'I – I just know. That's all.'

His voice became gentle. 'Jenna, if there's something you're not admitting you mustn't be afraid to tell me. You have to trust me. Have you ever heard of doctor-patient confidentiality rules? Anything you say in this office to me, anything you don't want revealed to anyone else, remains strictly between us.'

Jenna looked away. A full moment of silence passed. Then Dr Paley sighed deeply.

'Jenna, if you can't offer any explanation for your behaviour, then I have no alternative. You're demonstrating feelings of paranoia. You're talking to yourself. You're hearing voices. These actions are evidence of serious mental problems, the kind of problems we aren't capable of dealing with here at Harmony House.'

Jenna looked at him. 'What do you mean?'

'I'll have to consider recommending that you be sent to another facility.'

Jenna drew in her breath. 'What kind of facility?' she asked, but she had a sinking suspicion she already knew the answer to the question.

'An institution that can provide the kind of therapy we're not equipped to handle here.'

Jenna put it more bluntly. 'A nuthouse. You want to commit me to an insane asylum.'

'A mental hospital,' he corrected her. 'You've said you're not a juvenile delinquent, and I believe you. But you've got serious issues that need to be addressed.'

'I'm not crazy!' Jenna cried out. 'It's just that I'm different!'

'How?'

'Because – it's because – I can –' she clenched her fists. She couldn't say it. If he thought she was crazy now, what would he think if she told the truth?

'Tell me, Jenna,' he said urgently. 'What makes you different? Jenna, I don't want to send you to a mental hospital. But you have to give me an explanation, or I won't have any alternative. Tell me! What can you do?'

'I can read minds!' Jenna cried out. Then she buried her face in her hands.

It was out. She'd said it. And now he'd pick up the phone and call for an ambulance. She'd seen movies, she knew what would happen next. Men in white jackets would put her in a straitjacket and carry her away . . .

When nothing happened right away, she took her hands from her eyes. He was looking at her seriously, but she didn't see alarm in his eyes. It was more like interest . . .

'I knew there was more to your case than meets the eye, Jenna,' he said.

'You did?' she asked stupidly.

He nodded. 'I didn't know what, or why, but I could sense you had something extraordinary about you.'

Was he putting her on? Trying to make her dig a deeper hole to sink into?

'Why did you think that about me?' she asked.

'It's an instinct,' he said simply. 'Years of working with young people have given me a sense of what people are all about. You have a gift.'

'Why did you call it that?' she asked sharply.

He didn't answer. 'Tell me more about your gift.'

'It's just something I can do,' she replied.

She wanted to look away again, but there was something about his gaze that held her.

'What am I thinking about right now?' he asked.

Still suspicious, Jenna eyed him warily. Then she began to concentrate.

It was almost too easy, like he was putting his thoughts out there in writing, in big black and white letters. 'You're thinking about food. Chinese food. You're thinking about getting sweet and sour pork for lunch from a Chinese takeaway when you leave here.' After a second, she added, 'and cold sesame noodles.'

He nodded. 'Very good. You're absolutely right.'

'I know,' she said. But she thought his reaction was strangely calm. 'Aren't you shocked?'

'No,' he said. 'I've done a lot of research into these kinds of extrasensory abilities. Some people have gifts that simply can't be explained scientifically. There are people who can see into the future, people who can move things with their minds . . .'

'I can't do that,' Jenna said quickly.

But her expression must have told him something. 'Does this have anything to do with your special class, Jenna? The one called "Gifted"?'

Jenna didn't know what to say. It was one thing to give away her own secret. How could she betray her classmates?

'I can't talk about that,' she said.

He didn't press her. 'I understand.' He closed her

file. 'I'm going to look into this resident assistant. His name is Peter Blake, right? He cannot be permitted to continue in his position. His contract must be terminated immediately.'

'You said you'd keep my secret!' Jenna exclaimed.

'And I will,' the doctor assured her. 'I can investigate this without revealing my sources.'

'But he'll know it's me who told on him,' Jenna protested. 'The other kids – they don't mind what he's doing to them. He'll tell them it's me who got him fired. I could be in danger here!'

'I realize that,' he said. 'Which is why I'm going to recommend that you be given an early release from Harmony House.'

'An early release?' Jenna repeated in disbelief.

He nodded. 'There will be some paperwork involved. But I can make some calls, pull some strings. And with any luck, you'll be home tomorrow.'

Home. Tomorrow. Jenna gazed at him in wonderment. So Madame was wrong. There *were* people in this world who could be trusted with their secret gifts. Not many, of course.

But she'd just found one.

Chapter Twelve

TRACEY WAS WIPED OUT. Did invisibility drain her energy in some special, highly complicated cellular way? she wondered. No, she was pretty sure she was just normally exhausted. After all, other physical sensations remained behind when her physical self wasn't present. She got hungry, she got thirsty, she had headaches . . . why wouldn't she be tired? And even now, at ten o'clock in the morning, after spending the night in an unusually uncomfortable position, she had every right to be extremely beat.

When she left the house-of-the-bad-guys, it was almost one in the morning. She'd taken a few more photos with her phone, and then the group inside disbanded. Only Clare remained in the house. She must live there, Tracey thought.

She made her way back to her own home, and there

she encountered a problem she hadn't counted on. The house was dark, everyone was in bed, so she assumed she could walk right in. What she hadn't considered was the fact that her security-conscious parents would have locked the doors from the inside. And then it started to rain.

Invisibility did not protect her from natural forces, and Tracey felt cold and wet. She found shelter in the back yard, in the septuplets' playhouse. It was a bigger-than-average playhouse, but it hadn't been set up for sleeping, and Tracey had to attempt sleeping on a hard wood floor. This was not a restful experience.

Now, stiff and sleepy, she sat on the steps in front of Ken's house and tried not to doze off. The rain had stopped, there was actually some sunshine, and she figured Ken wouldn't stay inside all day. She just hoped he wasn't the type who slept till noon on weekends.

He wasn't. Just half an hour later, the front door opened and Ken emerged. Unfortunately, he wasn't alone. A man she assumed was his father walked alongside him and they headed towards the car on the drive.

'Ken!' she called. Ken stopped, turned and looked around.

'It's me, Tracey. I'm still invisible. I'm on your steps.'

'Ken?' his father asked. 'Are you coming?'

'Yeah, sure.' Ken mouthed some words. Tracey couldn't figure out exactly what he was telling her, but she knew from his fierce expression that it had to be something like 'shut up' or 'beat it'.

'Ken, it's important! I've found out something about the conspiracy. And I know who the real spy is. Ken, *please*, talk to me!'

He and his father had reached the car and Mr Preston was opening the door on the driver's side. But Ken didn't move.

'Ken, let's go!' his father said.

'Um . . . you go, Dad. I've changed my mind.'

His father looked confused. 'I thought you wanted me to drop you off at Mike's.'

'I'm going to take my bike. It's OK, you go on.'

His father still looked puzzled, but he shrugged, got into the car and took off. Ken waited until he was out of sight before he joined Tracey on the steps.

'I'm not sitting on you, am I?'

'Believe me, you'd know if you sat on me,' Tracey said. 'I still have feelings.'

'OK, so what's so important?'

'Look at this.' Tracey put her mobile phone down on the ground, where it magically appeared for Ken. 'Click on photos and tell me what you see.'

'Not a thing,' Ken replied. 'Your battery's dead.'

Tracey groaned. Of course, she hadn't been able to recharge it the night before. 'Well, I'll tell you. It's a photo of Carter with Clare, Serena, that Stuart Kelley guy . . . and Mr Jackson. *Our* Mr Jackson. And Carter's talking to them.'

She'd made an impression – she could see it on his face. She told him the whole story – how she'd followed Carter to the house and watched the proceedings through a window.

'He's the spy, Ken, not Amanda. That whole zombie business, it's a big act he's putting on. He sits in our class and pretends he can't communicate, then he goes and reports on us to these people. That's how Jackson knows about us. *He* put the knife in Jenna's locker because he was afraid she was reading his mind and he had to get her out of the picture.'

'How do you know that?' Ken asked.

She remembered her promise to Amanda. 'Well . . . it makes sense, doesn't it?' She hurried on. 'Other things make sense too, Ken. Like when we were kidnapped, Carter was taken first, remember? They got information out of him about the rest of us. Then, after they took me and Emily and the others, they sent him back because they didn't need him.'

Ken didn't say anything.

'Don't you believe me?' Tracey asked him.

'Are you sure about Jackson? You said yourself, you were looking through a window. Maybe it was someone who just looks like Mr Jackson. I mean, I'm not crazy about the guy, but he's the principal of a middle school, for crying out loud!'

'He's definitely involved with this conspiracy,' Tracey insisted. 'I'm not the only one who's seen him with those other creeps. Amanda said —' She caught herself just in time and stopped.

Ken rolled his eyes. 'I should have known Amanda had something to do with all this. Did you two cook up this story together?'

'Ken! Amanda is not the spy, I swear to you!'

'How can you be so sure about that?' he countered.

Frustrated, Tracey wanted to scream. *This* was exactly why a person shouldn't promise to keep secrets.

'You see?' Ken said triumphantly. 'You're not really sure, are you? You don't want to admit that Amanda can be this evil.'

'And you don't want to admit that you have a thing for her,' Tracey shot back. 'You're still upset that she didn't tell you about Serena in the seance. You're letting your personal feelings get in the way of logic, Ken!'

'That's bull,' Ken muttered.

'Oh, come on, Ken, get real! You like Amanda, you've always been into her. You're just trying to get back at her for not acting like she's into you! Which, by the way, I think she is.'

Ken looked away, as if he didn't want to confront something he knew was true.

'Talk to her,' Tracey pleaded. 'Tell her . . .' She tried to think of a way to clue him in without breaking her promise. 'Tell her to tell you what she told me.'

'Forget it,' Ken said. 'I'm not talking to her.' He stood up. 'I have to go.'

Helpless, Tracey watched him walk away. Now what? She was on her own.

Yawning, she decided to go home and get some sleep. There, she could plug in her phone, recharge it, and be all set to go back to Clare's house.

She didn't know the conspirators' schedule – if they met daily or if Carter met with them every night at midnight. But if Clare's house was their headquarters, there had to be items lying around which could provide evidence. So even if there was no gathering of bad guys, she'd accomplish something.

On her own. Totally on her own, by herself. And she was scared. OK, she was invisible. Nobody could really hurt her if she couldn't be seen, right? But even so, she was afraid.

She tried to shake off the fear and concentrate on her immediate task. First, she had to get into Clare's house. If there was no meeting and people weren't going in and out, how could she carry out any investigation? For that reason, she decided to go to Clare's earlier, in the afternoon, when hopefully the woman might leave or come home and open a door for her.

Reasonably refreshed, with her fear on a back burner and with a fully charged mobile phone, she left her room. She felt pretty focused, but even so, she couldn't help picking up on the family conversation going on in the living room.

For once, the Devon Seven were quiet. Her parents were talking to them.

'Girls, we know you miss Tracey,' her father was saying. 'Your mother and I miss her too. But even if we can't see her, we know that she's here.'

Her mother spoke up. 'George, you're confusing them. They can't understand Tracey's gift.'

Tracey had to smile. Her mother was right – how could the five-year-olds understand her gift, when she couldn't understand it herself? Impulsively, out of the septuplets' eye range, she picked up her mother's handbag. The sudden disappearance of her bag caught the woman's attention. Tracey then placed it back down. Her mother smiled.

'But you don't have to worry, girls,' she said. 'Tracey's all right.'

Was she? Tracey wondered. Was she really all right?

She'd never been invisible for this long before, and although she hadn't tried to reappear today, she had the feeling it wouldn't work if she did. And here she was, all alone, ready to embark on what could possibly be a very dangerous mission. She didn't know *what* she was.

All she knew for sure was that she'd made a promise to Jenna, to get her out of that awful place. She needed to be able to prove Jenna's innocence, and from what Amanda had told her the evidence could only come from Mr Jackson.

It took her a while to find Clare's house. And when she thought she'd found it she was actually at the house next door. She realized this when a car pulled into the other house's drive and Clare got out.

Tracey tore across the lawn, determined not to get shut out this time. Clare was talking on her mobile phone, and when Tracey caught up to her she was able to hear her side of the conversation.

'I'm telling you, she's been released! No, I don't know why, but we have to talk about this, today. And bring the kid.'

There was a pause.

'Good grief, you're the principal, you can come up with an excuse. Tell the parents it's a special school activity or something. Or you're taking him to see a specialist. Come up with something – just get over here.'

The kid – she had to be talking about Carter, Tracey thought. And the 'she' who was released – was that Jenna? Had she left Harmony House? Clare shut off her phone as she went into the house and Tracey slipped in alongside her.

Clare went through the living room, but Tracey paused and gazed around. It looked like such an ordinary living room – there was a modern sofa, a couple of chairs, a coffee table, but the only piece of furniture that grabbed her eye was a desk.

She went on through the dining room and spotted Clare in the kitchen. She was making coffee and Tracey hoped she wasn't going to bring it into the living room. Clare might not be able to see her, but if Tracey wanted to open drawers, or move things about, she needed to do it when Clare wasn't around.

She eased open the desk's file drawer slowly, trying not to make any noise. A row of folders greeted her and she knelt down to read the tabs on them. Bills . . . receipts . . . banking . . . They were the same labels she'd see if she opened her parents' desk at home. Except for one.

She was amazed to see that Clare hadn't even tried to disguise the subject of the folder. It was right there, printed in black ink on a white tab: Gifted.

She went to take another quick look at the kitchen. Clare was sitting at a little kitchen table with her cup of coffee and she'd opened a newspaper. It looked like she'd be occupied for a while.

She pulled the folder out and set it on the desk. Taking a deep breath, she opened it.

The first page could have been some sort of application form. It bore the heading: Amanda Beeson. A small head-and-shoulders photo of her classmate was attached. It looked like it could have been a recent school photo.

Data about Amanda included her address, phone number, parents' names and occupations. Date and place of birth. Then there was physical information.

Height: 5'2".

Weight: 110 lb.

Hair: Light brown.

Eyes: Blue.

So far, this could have come directly from some file at Meadowbrook Middle School.

But the next piece of information was something Tracey never expected to see neatly typed in black and white on an official-looking document.

Gift: Ability to transfer consciousness into another body.

Characteristics: Subject must experience a sensation of pity for the person in the body prior to transfer. Subject is without personal consciousness, but remains physically unchanged, with all natural abilities intact. Subject appears to be operating through a remote memory of typical behaviour patterns. All consciousness of the subject is in the new body. Consciousness of person who normally inhabits body appears to be in a sleeping state.

Limitations: Subject exhibits some control in taking over a body, but has not yet achieved the ability to release body at will.

Project potential: Could replace heads of state and others in a position of decision-making in order to establish an environment suitable for project.

Tracey turned the page. The next document was devoted to Martin. There was all the basic information, but Tracey ignored that.

Gift: Ability to develop super strength.

Limitations: Subject must feel ridiculed for strength to emerge.

Project potential: Battle.

She read Jenna's page next.

Gift: Ability to read thoughts of other human beings.

Characteristics: Subject must want to read the thoughts and must be able to concentrate. Object of mind-reading will not be aware of the process.

Limitations: Subject appears to be able to employ gift at will. Object who is aware of subject's gift may be able to mentally block the process.

Project potential: Ability to determine loyalties and emotional states. Revelation of confidential information. Verification of intent.

Verification of intent . . . Tracey assumed that was just a fancy way of saying Jenna would know if someone was telling the truth.

The document devoted to Sarah was particularly intriguing. Under limitations, it stated: Subject has personal reasons for not wishing to exercise her gift. Must ascertain the nature of the reasons and resolve her reluctance so that gift may be exploited. And under Project potential, there was only one word: Unlimited.

There was a knock on the door. Hastily, she closed the folder and shoved it back in the file. She barely got the drawer closed before Clare entered the room and went to the door.

Serena-the-student-teacher-alias-Cassandra-the-medium was at the door, along with the man Tracey knew as Stuart Kelley.

'What's so important that we had to come rushing over here?' Serena demanded to know.

'It's the Kelley girl. She left Harmony House this morning.'

Stuart's eyebrows shot up. 'She escaped?'

'No, she was released early.'

'Why?' the man asked.

'I don't know,' Clare replied. 'The investigator just knew she'd left. I'm hoping the kid knows something.'

'How could he know anything already?' Serena asked. 'It's Saturday – there's no school.'

Clare ignored her. 'Here they come now.'

Mr Jackson and Carter arrived and within seconds they were all at the dining-room table. Jackson looked tense. Carter had no expression at all. Tracey took out her mobile phone and began moving around the table, snapping photos.

'I can't have her back at the school,' Mr Jackson said flatly. 'She's too dangerous. I can't be constantly thinking about what I'm thinking about.'

'But you can block her,' Clare pointed out.

'Not if I don't see her,' he said. 'She's got a way of sneaking around. I've got over three hundred students at the school, I've got people running in and out of my office all day. I can't know where she is every minute.'

'I don't understand why you're so anxious about her,' Serena said. 'You don't even know for sure if she's interested in reading your mind.'

'I didn't like the way she was looking at me in the office the other day,' Jackson grumbled.

'You're the principal – it's natural for her to hate you,' Stuart said. 'A kid like her, she hates any kind of authority. Look, I know her better than the rest of you. I was almost her father. Just because she gives you dirty looks doesn't mean she knows anything about you.'

'These kids aren't idiots,' Jackson declared. 'They're going to put two and two together. They know you were a fraud. They know Clare's out to get them, they're suspicious of Serena . . . They're going to start connecting the dots.'

Clare interrupted. 'But they don't know about you. They have no idea you're involved.'

'I'm not so sure about that,' Jackson muttered. 'The Beeson girl – she's working in my office. She could be snooping around.'

Serena frowned. 'Which one is she?'

'The body snatcher,' Clare told her.

Serena's face cleared. 'Oh, right. She came to one of my seances with Ken.'

Clare's eyebrows went up. 'You didn't tell us that.'

Serena shrugged. 'It was only the one time – she never showed up again.'

But Clare still looked disturbed. She turned to Carter, who hadn't said a word. 'Did Amanda say anything about the seance in class?'

In Tracey's view, Carter looked exactly the way he would look if someone at school asked him a direct question. He just stared into space, not even acknowledging that he'd been addressed.

Clare appeared irritated. 'Haven't you brought him out yet?' she asked Serena.

'You haven't given me a chance, have you?' Serena snapped. She pulled her chair around so she could face Carter directly. She stared at him, so hard that Tracey could actually see her pupils enlarge. She didn't blink at all. Then she began murmuring softly. Tracey couldn't make out the words.

She spoke directly into the boy's ear, her voice soft and rhythmic. Tracey moved closer, but even when she was practically on top of them, she couldn't understand what Serena was saying. It was like gibberish, the same nonsense words over and over in a monotonous tone.

It was a good thing nobody here could hear her, because her gasp would have been audible. The change in Carter's expression was dramatic. It was like a curtain had been lifted from his eyes. She hadn't been able to see this when she watched through the window last night, so she was completely startled.

'We want to ask you about Amanda,' Serena said to him. 'She came to one of the seances. Did she say anything about it in class?'

For the first time, Tracey heard Carter's voice. It was slightly high-pitched, which made him sound very young. But other than that, it was normal.

'Not just one seance,' he said. 'She went to all of them. Amanda was Margaret.'

Serena drew in her breath sharply. 'Amanda took over Margaret's body?'

'Yes,' Carter replied. 'She felt sorry for her. She didn't want to be Margaret, but it happened.'

'Margaret . . .' Jackson repeated, and frowned. Serena turned to him.

'My friend, who was helping me out. She pretended to have just lost her mother. She came to a meeting – you met her. She was freaked out, she couldn't handle that stay in jail. She was a nervous wreck, remember?'

'Whatever happened to her?' Stuart asked.

'She had some sort of breakdown and she's living with her parents in Florida.' Suddenly, Serena gasped.

'Ohmigod, it's all starting to make sense! Her behaviour at the seance . . .'

It dawned on Tracey that she should be recording this conversation. Hurriedly, she fumbled with her mobile phone, looking for the little icon that would turn the phone into a recorder . . .

And it slipped out of her hand.

'What's that?' Clare asked.

They were all staring at a mobile phone, which had suddenly appeared on the floor. Serena reached down and picked it up.

'It's not mine,' she said.

Tracey tried not to panic. OK, they had her phone. They'd see the pictures she'd taken. They might even be able to figure out that the phone belonged to her. But it wasn't like they could do anything to her – they couldn't even see her . . .

Then her stomach turned over. Because they weren't looking at the phone any more. They were looking right at her. And they could see her.

Chapter Thirteen

Jenna's mother was trying very hard to grasp the situation. 'But why would the principal want to get rid of you, Jenna? You haven't been in any trouble since you started at Meadowbrook.'

'He's afraid of me, Mom,' Jenna explained. 'Because I can read minds. I don't know what he's thinking about that's so bad, but he doesn't want me to find out.'

'Why don't you just tell him you won't read his mind?' Mrs Kelley suggested.

'I don't think he'd believe me,' Jenna said.

'Oh, dear,' her mother sighed. 'Jenna, couldn't you just stop reading minds? It's not really a very nice habit, is it?'

Jenna smiled. Her mother meant well, but she was no Dr Paley. She'd never be able to understand.

The doorbell rang. 'That must be Emily,' Mrs Kelley said. 'She called earlier and I told her you were coming home.'

But it was a different classmate who stood in the doorway.

'Ken!'

'Emily called and told me you were home,' he said. 'I have to talk to you about something.'

'Come on in. Mom, this is Ken Preston, from my class at Meadowbrook.'

'Hello, Ken,' her mother said brightly. 'Would you kids like something to eat? There are cookies . . .'

'No, thank you, Mrs Kelley,' Ken said politely. 'I just need to talk to Jenna about something. I won't stay long.'

'I'll give you two some privacy,' Mrs Kelley said, and disappeared into the kitchen.

'She's nice,' Ken said.

Jenna nodded. She could remember a time when she would never have willingly allowed a classmate to meet her mother. She could also remember a time when the mere notion of Ken Preston showing up on her doorstep would have boggled her mind.

Now she wasn't boggled, but she was puzzled. 'What's up?'

'Tracey's been invisible for a while,' he began.

Jenna nodded. 'I know. She came to see me at Harmony House.'

'Well, she came to see me this morning. And she says . . .' He frowned. 'This is going to sound crazy. She claims she spied on a meeting. That Clare woman, Serena, the guy who said he was your father . . . and Mr Jackson!'

Slowly, Jenna nodded. 'That doesn't sound so crazy to me.'

'But you haven't heard the rest of it. She says Carter's the spy, not Amanda. She says she actually saw him talking at this meeting.'

'Wow!' Jenna breathed. 'I wouldn't have guessed *that*.'

'You believe her?' Ken asked.

'Tracey doesn't lie, Ken.'

Ken frowned. 'She said I should talk to Amanda. And to ask Amanda to tell me what she told her. Does that make sense to you?'

'Yeah.'

Ken pulled out his mobile and just looked at it for a moment. 'She's gotta hate me. I mean, I haven't exactly been very nice to her.' Then, with a less-than-enthusiastic expression, he hit a number.

Jenna grinned. 'You got her on speed-dial, huh?'

'Forgot to take her off,' he mumbled. 'Hello, Amanda? This is Ken. Yeah. Um . . . are you busy? I mean, like, could I come by and talk to you about something? OK.'

He put the phone back in his pocket. 'I'm going over there now.'

Jenna grabbed her jacket. 'I'm going with you.'

He didn't protest. In fact, Jenna could have sworn she saw relief in his eyes. She couldn't blame him. She wouldn't want to face an irate Amanda alone either.

And she was glad Ken was by her side when Amanda opened the door. The look Amanda gave Jenna was a lot scarier than the one she gave Ken.

'What's *she* doing here?' Amanda wanted to know.

'Don't worry, Amanda, I'm not armed,' Jenna said.

Amanda sniffed, but she stepped aside and let them both in. Before Ken could say anything, she made a statement.

'I am *not* the spy.'

'I know, I know,' Ken said. 'Tracey told me.'

That didn't seem to make Amanda any happier. 'Oh, so you believe Tracey but you wouldn't believe *me*.'

'I *want* to believe you, Amanda!' Ken exclaimed. 'It's just that, I don't know, you get me all mixed up!' Suddenly, his face was red. Jenna had the feeling he'd just admitted something he didn't want to say.

And Amanda went pink. 'You mix me up too!' she blurted out. 'I mean . . . Oh, never mind, just forget it.'

Ken looked like he was about to smile, but then thought better of it. 'Well, for cryin' out loud, Amanda, what was I supposed to think? I find out you were at that seance all the time, knowing full well that it was a scam, but you let me go on and make a fool of myself believing that woman was a real medium. I was pretty pissed off at you!'

'Aw, you can't blame her, Ken,' Jenna broke in. 'She got to be a twenty-five-year-old woman for a weekend. It opened up new shopping opportunities.'

Amanda glared at her, and Jenna actually backed down.

'Sorry. I'm sure you had other reasons.'

'No kidding. Look, I know what you guys think of me. You think my gift is worthless and I only think about myself. I wanted to show you that maybe I had something to offer. Like, I could find out more about these people who are out to get us. And I did.'

'What did you find out?' Ken asked.

Amanda smirked. 'Wouldn't you like to know.'

'Oh, go ahead and tell him, Amanda,' Jenna said.

Amanda narrowed her eyes. 'Did Tracey tell you? She promised to keep it a secret.'

'She didn't have to tell me. I read her mind.'

'She wouldn't tell me either,' Ken said. 'Tracey told me to ask you to tell me what you told her.' He grimaced. 'Did that make sense?'

'I guess so,' Amanda replied with clear reluctance. She paused dramatically. Jenna had an enormous urge to scream, 'Spill the beans, Amanda,' but she managed to keep her mouth shut. She knew the girl would want to make the most of this moment.

First, they had to hear the tale of her two hours in jail as Margaret, her desperate attempts to get back into her own body, her fear of never seeing the light of day again, blah, blah, blah. Someone bailed both her and

Serena/Cassandra out of jail, and they went immediately to a meeting in a nondescript suburban house on an ordinary tree-lined street.

'And there they were at the dining table, the conspirators,' Amanda said. 'Clare, the kidnapper. Stuart Kelley. *And . . .*' she paused dramatically.

Jenna couldn't stand it any longer. 'Mr Jackson.'

Amanda's eyes shot daggers at her, but she was distracted and rewarded with Ken's wide-eyed reaction.

'So it *is* true?'

Amanda nodded solemnly. 'He's one of them, Ken. The second I saw him, the shock sent me right back into myself. But I decided I was going to find out more about this. That's why I took the job in his office, so I could spy on him. On *Mr Jackson*, Ken. Not you guys.'

Ken offered a weak smile. 'OK, I was wrong about you. I'm sorry.'

Amanda affected the look of a martyr. 'I just wanted to prove to you all that I could do something to help us.'

'Did it ever occur to you that we could have all worked together and accomplished more?' Jenna asked.

Amanda made a face at her. 'Look who's talking. Miss Sociability. Since when have you been into teamwork?'

'Since I came to grips with reality,' Jenna shot back. 'You should give it a try sometime.' She turned to Ken.

'Can I use your phone? I want to make some calls.'

CHAPTER FOURTEEN

HOW LONG HAD SHE been here? Lying on a bed, Tracey stared at the ceiling and realized that she'd completely lost track of time. She had a vague memory of being brought into this bedroom, but when? She felt dizzy and disoriented. Had they given her some kind of drug? Or was she just suffering from the shock of suddenly finding herself made of flesh and blood and bones again?

The clouds in her head began to float away and she started thinking more clearly. Serena had probably hypnotized her, and she was just now coming out of it.

She was quite a hypnotist, that Serena. Tracey always thought hypnosis could only happen if the subject cooperated, if the subject was willing to be put under. Tracey certainly hadn't given permission.

And what kind of hypnosis had she been using on Carter? From what she'd observed, it was like he was in a constant state of hypnosis, and she brought him out of it only when they wanted information.

But all these questions could be put on hold. Right now she had to concentrate on getting out of there.

She got off the bed and grabbed on to a bedpost as a fresh wave of dizziness swept over her. Her legs were trembling too. But the sensations passed, and she made her way to the door. She wasn't surprised to find it locked. Of course, she was being held prisoner. And even if she went invisible, she couldn't get through a locked door.

But they'd come in here sooner or later, she assumed, and if she was invisible, she could slip out while the door was open. She tried to concentrate, to pull up the feelings that could make her disappear.

You're worthless, you're alone, nobody sees you, nobody cares about you, you're depressed . . .

It wasn't working – she was still all there. Maybe Serena had given her some post-hypnotic suggestion . . .

There were windows in the bedroom. She went over to them and examined the latches.

With the sound of a lock turning, she faced the door. Clare stood there. 'What are you doing?'

What could Tracey say – 'Admiring the view?' It was a stupid question.

'I'm trying to get out,' she replied.

'Well, you can't,' Clare said. 'Come with me.'

The others were still at the dining-room table. 'You're slipping, Serena,' Clare announced as she pushed Tracey towards the table. 'She's already awake.'

Serena frowned. 'It's not easy with these kids. They're not normal, their brains don't work like other people's. I'm going to have to develop some sort of special individualized hypnotic programme for each of them.'

Stuart indicated Carter. 'You didn't have any problem with *him*.'

Serena gave him a withering look. 'Of course not. He isn't gifted.'

Now, that was interesting, Tracey thought. She'd always wondered about that. So he hadn't been put in their class because he was like the rest of them. He'd been placed there simply because he was strange, weird, not normal. Which, when she thought about it, *was* like the rest of them . . .

Stuart was looking at her nervously. 'Is she trying to disappear?'

'She shouldn't be able to,' Serena said. 'I gave her a post-hypnotic suggestion.'

Clare grimaced. 'What makes you think that's going to work any more efficiently than your hypnosis?'

'I'd like to see *you* do a better job,' Serena retorted.

Mr Jackson spoke up. 'Don't bicker. We need to concentrate on how we can make this work for us.'

'What's the problem?' Stuart asked. 'We were going to take them all eventually anyway.'

'But not yet,' Clare snapped. 'Nothing's in place. We're not ready for her.'

They were talking about her like she wasn't there. In a way, this could be good for her, though. If she could feel like she wasn't there, maybe in another moment or two she *wouldn't* be there.

But instead of feeling depressed, she felt annoyed with them. Did they think she was stupid? 'Are you talking about the project?' she blurted out.

That got their attention. 'What do you know about the project?' Clare asked sharply.

Uh-oh! Tracey offered a weak smile, and hoped it looked mysterious.

'I don't like this,' Stuart declared. 'She knows too much.'

'And she could disappear any minute,' Clare added.

Serena agreed. 'So what are we going to do with her?'

Only Mr Jackson seemed calm. 'She's not going to disappear.'

'How can we stop her?' Stuart wanted to know.

Mr Jackson's smile was extremely unpleasant. 'I'm going to tell her exactly what will happen if she does.' He addressed Tracey directly.

'Do you love your little sisters, Tracey?'

Tracey stared at him blankly.

'And what about your parents, Tracey? Do you love them?'

Mutely, she nodded.

'And you wouldn't want anything terrible to happen to them, would you?'

Tracey found her voice, but it was trembling. 'You're a very bad person.'

Mr Jackson shrugged. 'Good, bad – it's all relative.'

'Besides,' Tracey continued, trying very hard to steady her voice, 'I can't always control my gift. Do you think I wanted to appear in front of you today?'

'But you're getting better and better,' Mr Jackson said. 'That's what your special class is all about, isn't it?' He nodded towards Carter. 'That's what he's told us. You practise, you work at gaining control. Madame's doing a good job with you, isn't she?'

Tracey could feel her own breathing become harder, faster. Was it possible that Madame was involved in the conspiracy? The one person they all completely trusted, the one who knew them better than their own families – was she part of this? Her heart was thumping and she couldn't catch her breath.

'She's hyperventilating,' Clare declared in disgust.

'It's a panic attack,' Serena said. 'Get a paper bag.'

The next thing Tracey knew, her mouth was covered with a bag and someone was yelling, 'Deep breaths! Deep breaths!' Her heart pounded harder, louder, she could hear the banging . . .

But the banging wasn't coming from her chest. Someone was rapping on the door.

'Quiet!' Mr Jackson ordered them. In a softer voice, he asked, 'Is the door locked?'

'Of course,' Clare whispered back.

But the door opened anyway. Mr Jackson raced towards it and collided with a speeding wheelchair.

It got him right in the stomach. 'Ow!' he screamed.

But none of his comrades raced to his aid. They were all frozen as they watched the rest of the rescue team march in and close the door behind them.

Tracey felt her breathing ease as she took in the new arrivals. Ken, Jenna and Amanda followed Charles. Emily, Martin and Sarah came in next. Madame brought up the rear.

Serena began chanting at Carter, and the boy's eyes were becoming even more glazed than they were normally. Tracey suddenly realized that she might be trying to hypnotize him permanently, so that he couldn't ever testify against them.

'Charles!' Tracey yelled, and pointed towards the hypnotist. But Charles only glanced at Serena. He focused on the paper bag that had been used on Tracey, and sent it flying across the room. It fell over Serena's head and covered her face. But Serena continued to chant.

'I'm going to have to knock her out,' Charles declared.

Tracey looked around the room. She didn't see anything particularly heavy. 'With what?'

Charles grinned. Suddenly, a big frying pan sailed into the room. It flew through space towards Serena. Since she couldn't see it coming, she couldn't duck – and it hit her in the head. *That* stopped her chanting.

Martin gasped. 'Where did that pan come from?'

'From the kitchen,' Charles said with a smug expression. 'I don't have to see things to move them any more.'

Madame was clearly impressed. 'Charles, you're improving!' But her attention was diverted when Stuart Kelley began moving towards the door. She turned to Sarah.

'Make him stop!'

But Sarah looked absolutely terrified, and didn't move.

'Martin, stop him!' Jenna yelled.

Martin cringed. Jenna groaned, and spoke rapidly.

'Oh, that's right, I forgot – you're a weakling, you're hopeless, you can't do anything, you puny feeble little nobody.'

Martin went into action. Seconds later, Stuart Kelley was on the ground, knocked unconscious. Jenna looked down at his prone body.

'Hi, *Daddy*,' she said sarcastically. 'What's new?'

Clare stood very still, taking in the scene. Then she started towards the kitchen. Jenna watched her.

'Don't even think about it,' she said. 'Charles can get a weapon out of your hand before you can get a firm grip on it. He could even turn it around and use it on *you*.'

Charles's eyes widened. 'Gee, you're right! I never thought of that.'

Mr Jackson had recovered from his encounter with the wheelchair. He stood there stiffly, and spoke to Madame.

'What do you think you're going to do now?'

'I've called the police,' she replied. 'And when they arrive, I'll accuse you of kidnapping Tracey.'

'We didn't kidnap Tracey,' Clare objected. 'She came here of her own free will.'

'Then I'll accuse you of kidnapping Carter,' the teacher said.

Mr Jackson didn't blink. 'Call his foster parents. He has their permission to be with me. You have no proof of anything illegal going on here, Madame. And I sincerely doubt that you really called the police.' He actually smiled.

Jenna whispered in Tracey's ear. 'She didn't. She's just trying to scare him.'

The principal continued. 'It seems to me, Madame, that you have more to fear from the police than we do.'

'What do you mean?' she asked.

'I'm the principal of Meadowbrook Middle School. I'm a respected member of this community. If you have me arrested, there will be publicity. And I'll have a platform to tell the world all about your Gifted class.'

Tracey looked at Madame. Was that fear in her eyes? If so, it vanished quickly.

'And I'll have no option but to instruct my students to use their gifts against you. You know what they can do.' As if to make her point even clearer, she put a hand on Sarah's shoulder. Sarah flinched, but she didn't contradict Madame.

Mr Jackson fell silent for a moment. 'Then it looks like perhaps we should make a deal,' he said finally.

'Go on,' Madame said.

'You say nothing to anyone about this. And I won't expose your students.'

Ken spoke. 'That's not much of a deal. He wouldn't tell people about us, Madame. It's like you always say – nobody believes we have gifts.'

'And why would the police believe *you*?' Clare countered. 'You have no evidence against us.'

'But there *is* evidence,' Tracey cried out. 'You can tell the police about the project. You can show them the plans.'

'What project?' Madame asked.

'It's what they want to use us for. It's in a folder, in that desk.'

'I'll get it,' Charles said quickly. He looked at the desk, and all the drawers opened. And all the papers came flying out. Telephone bills, bank statements – hundreds of documents floated through the air.

'Oops!' Charles murmured. 'Sorry.'

'The police are here!' Emily announced.

'Madame, they'll see Serena,' Ken pointed out.

'Sarah, move Serena,' Madame ordered.

There was a knock on the door. 'Police! Open up!'

Mr Jackson turned to Clare.

'Open the door.'

'Sarah!' Madame exclaimed. 'Do it!'

But Serena remained where she was, with the paper bag on her head and unconscious. And Clare was already beginning to open the door.

'Sarah, quick!' Madame hissed.

'Oh, Madame,' the girl whispered in an agonized voice. But she looked at Serena. And as if by her own free will, the woman got up and walked out of the room into the kitchen.

Two police officers stood in the doorway. 'Excuse me, ma'am,' one of them said to Clare. 'But we've had a complaint of some kind of disruption going on here.'

The other officer looked at the papers lying all over the floor. 'What's going on here?'

Mr Jackson strode forward. 'Good afternoon, officers.' He introduced himself and shook their hands. One of the officers looked at him with interest.

'We've met before. You're my kid's school principal.'

'That's right,' Mr Jackson said, beaming. 'We're working on a school project here.' He looked at the papers and smiled ruefully. 'I'm afraid we had a little accident and made a mess. But I don't quite think it's in the category of anything criminal!' He laughed at his own little quip.

The police officers didn't laugh, but they didn't seem concerned either. 'I guess you made some noise and a neighbour complained,' one said. 'Just keep it down, OK?'

'Of course, officers,' Mr Jackson said smoothly.

Madame spoke up. 'Actually, the meeting has ended and we were about to leave. Come along, everyone.'

Eight of the nine gifted students gathered around her.

'Come along, Carter,' Madame called.

'No, Madame,' Jenna whispered frantically in her ear. 'He's the spy!'

But the teacher ignored her. 'Carter?' she called again.

In zombie mode, the boy rose from his seat at the dining table and joined them. Madame ushered them all past the policemen and out of the door.

She turned back to the people still in the house and spoke.

'This was an interesting meeting. Highly enlightening.' She paused, and then added, 'I'll get back to you, Mr Jackson, and we can continue negotiations.'

Chapter Fifteen

AS THE LAST CLASS period began on Monday afternoon, Room 209 was unusually quiet. Everyone seemed to be lost in their own thoughts as they waited for Madame to arrive.

There had been rumours and phone calls the day before and whispered conversations in the hallways of Meadowbrook today. But no one knew what was really going on.

Ken spoke quietly to Tracey. 'So you didn't find out what this project is all about.'

Tracey shook her head. 'I didn't get that far.'

Amanda had overheard them. Her comment was directed to Emily. 'Why can't you just look into the future and tell us?'

'I don't even know what to look for,' Emily told her. 'I have to know what the project *is* before I can see if it's going to happen.'

'Well, I'll never be able to read it in their minds,' Jenna grumbled. 'Not if they know I'm around.' She turned to Tracey. 'Too bad we can't combine our gifts.'

'Maybe we can figure out a way,' Tracey said. 'Do you guys realize, this was the first time we've all pooled our gifts? Everyone did something.' She ticked them off on her fingers. 'I got into the house, Charles made the locked door open. Martin stopped Stuart from escaping, Jenna read Clare's mind, Emily told us the police had arrived, and, and, oh yeah, Sarah moved Serena out of the dining room before the police could see her.'

'Yeah, right,' Jenna muttered. 'After Madame asked her *three* times.'

'But she did it,' Tracey said stoutly, and she smiled at Sarah. 'Thanks, Sarah.'

'You're welcome,' Sarah whispered, but she didn't seem proud of it and she looked away.

Amanda was offended. 'You left me out. I provided the information about Mr Jackson.'

Which Tracey could have provided, but she let Amanda take the credit. 'That's right.'

'And you left out Ken,' Amanda added. She smiled warmly at the boy.

Tracey grinned. So that 'sort-of' relationship was on again. 'Ken did a lot.'

'Not with my gift,' Ken said. He turned slightly, and eyed the small boy at the back. 'What about him?'

Silence fell over the room again as they all turned to look at Carter.

'It wasn't his fault,' Tracey declared. 'He was hypnotized.' But the looks that Carter was receiving from his classmates were less than friendly. The boy, as always – almost always – seemed oblivious. But now they all knew he took in everything they said, everything that happened in the class. They could never trust him.

Madame walked in. She wasn't alone.

'Good afternoon, class. I'd like to introduce Doctor Paley. He'd like to say a few words to you.'

The plump, balding man faced them. 'Hello. I met one of your classmates recently. She told me about her gift.'

A gasp went up from practically every student.

Jenna groaned. 'Knock it off, guys. It was me, OK?

I had to tell him or I'd have got tossed into a mental institution. But I didn't tell him about anyone else.'

'That's right,' the man said. 'Logic tells me that you all must be special in some way, but I have no idea what your gifts are, and I'm not going to ask you about them. Maybe, someday, you'll trust me and you'll want to tell me. But I won't be pressing you for information.'

Charles looked suspicious. 'Why are you here if you're not trying to find out stuff about us?'

'I'm here because you have a classmate in need,' he said simply.

'Carter,' Madame called softly. 'Could you come up here, please?'

Obediently, the boy rose and came to the front of the room. He stood silently by her desk.

'I have permission to take Carter back to Harmony House,' Dr Paley said. 'I'm going to try to help him there.'

'Just keep him away from the rest of us,' Charles said bitterly. 'He's a traitor.'

'Don't jump to conclusions,' Madame said. 'It may turn out that Carter can help us.'

'He doesn't have a gift,' Tracey told her.

Madame smiled. 'There are gifts, and there are gifts. There's a lot we don't know about Carter. Thank you, Doctor Paley.'

The doctor left with Carter. As soon as the door closed behind them, people had questions.

'Can we trust that Paley guy?' Charles wanted to know.

'He got me out of Harmony House,' Jenna replied. 'He's OK – I read his mind.'

'But what if Carter tells him everything about us?' Emily asked anxiously.

The conversation was stopped by a shrill buzz from the intercom on the wall behind Madame's desk. Then they heard the voice of Ms Simmons, the office secretary.

'May I have your attention? I have an important announcement to make. The Board of Education regrets to inform you that your principal, Mr Jackson, will be leaving his position due to personal reasons. Mr Jones from the History Department will be acting principal until the position is filled. I am sure you all join me in bidding Mr Jackson a fond farewell, and offering him our best wishes for future success.'

The intercom went silent, and silence remained in the classroom. But only for a few seconds. Then a couple of people let out a cheer, and everyone was talking at once.

'Was that part of the deal, Madame?'

'Is he leaving town?'

'Where's he going?'

'Does this mean we're safe?'

Madame rapped on her desk, and the voices died down.

'This isn't the end,' she said. Her voice was calm, but serious. 'And there's no reason to cheer. Mr Jackson is only one piece of what I think may be a very big puzzle. Even if he's out of the picture, you are not safe. There will be more challenges, bigger challenges, and we have to get ready to face them.'

'What kind of challenges?' Jenna asked.

'I don't know,' Madame replied simply.

'Then how can we get ready if we don't know what we're going to face?' Ken wanted to know.

'We're going to work on the gifts,' Madame said. 'Harder and faster than we've ever worked before. It's not simply a question of control any more, of fitting in, of being comfortable. You're never going to be like other people, and there's no point in trying. It's a question of getting better at being yourself.'

'I'm getting better,' Martin piped up. 'At that house, Jenna barely had to tease me at all to make my gift come out.'

'That's true,' Jenna admitted.

Madame nodded. 'Yes, you're improving, Martin. You're all improving. But you can't just get a little better. You have to find the extent of your gifts – your true potential.' She paused, and gazed at the room.

'You can't waste your gifts on trivialities.' She looked at Charles.

'Or run away from your gift.' She looked at Ken.

'Or fear it.' She looked at Sarah.

'Or—'

She was interrupted by the opening of the door. Tracey caught her breath. Mr Jackson was standing there.

'Just wanted to say goodbye,' he said, and smiled broadly. Nobody smiled back.

Madame eyed him evenly. 'Stay away from us.'

'Oh, I will,' he assured her. 'That's part of the deal.

But you know, Madame . . . you can't protect them for ever.' He was still smiling as he retreated and shut the door.

Madame turned to the class. 'You won't need protection, from me or anyone else. OK, let's move on. Are you ready?'

Heads were bobbing. Madame smiled a little sadly.

'No, you're not. But you will be.'

Tracey wanted to believe her. But deep in her heart she knew that in the end they only had to believe in themselves.

GIFTED

Out of Sight, Out of Mind

MARILYN KAYE

ONE MORNING AMANDA LOOKED IN
THE MIRROR AND ANOTHER GIRL
LOOKED BACK ...

Amanda Beeson is Queen Bee at Meadowbrook
Middle School. If you're not friends with Amanda,
you're nobody. But one morning gorgeous, popular
Amanda Beeson looks in the mirror and sees a very
different face staring back at her. The Queen Bee is
about to get a taste of life in someone else's shoes.

A selected list of titles available from Macmillan Children's Books

The prices shown below are correct at the time of going to press. However, Macmillan Publishers reserves the right to show new retail prices on covers, which may differ from those previously advertised.

All Pan Macmillan titles can be ordered from our website, www.panmacmillan.com, or from your local bookshop and are also available by post from:

Bookpost, PO Box 29, Douglas, Isle of Man IM99 1BQ

Credit cards accepted. For details:
Telephone: 01624 677237
Fax: 01624 670923
Email: bookshop@enterprise.net
www.bookpost.co.uk

Free postage and packing in the United Kingdom